# Eight Years

Penelope Smith

Copyright © 2024 by Penelope Smith

All rights reserved.

No portion of this book may be reproduced in any form without written permission from the publisher or author, except as permitted by U.S. copyright law.

# Contents


| | |
|---|---|
| Chapter One: | 1 |
| Chapter Two: | 14 |
| Chapter Three: | 35 |
| Chapter Four: | 74 |
| Chapter Five: | 79 |
| Chapter Six: | 88 |
| Chapter Seven: | 104 |
| Chapter Eight: | 116 |
| Chapter Nine: | 124 |
| Chapter Ten: | 134 |
| Chapter Eleven: | 141 |
| Chapter Twelve: | 150 |
| Chapter Thirteen: | 158 |
| Chapter Fourteen: | 168 |
| Chapter Fifteen: | 179 |

Chapter Sixteen:          192

Chapter Seventeen:        205

Chapter Eighteen:         214

Chapter Nineteen:         220

# Chapter One:

------------------------------------------------------------

I fiddled with the hem of my denim shorts and sighed.

"You ready?" My older brother, Chase asked me, pulling his leather cut on.

"I guess." I looked away from him.

"Be nice Parker, he's been away for a long time, he doesn't need to deal with your shit." Chase frowned lightly.

"Let's just go." I rolled my eyes and walked outside and into Chase's black Range Rover.

He climbed in beside me and started the car, pulling away from the mansion with another black Range Rover following us.

Chase ran an MC gang, before him, our father had ran it, then my grandfather and so on. Our dad, Alex Greyson had died when I was fifteen, he had been killed in a gang war and Chase had taken over ever since then. He was good at running the MC, it was all he knew, all he had been trained for.

I peaked over at him, his bright blue eyes were trained on the road ahead of him and his shaggy dark blonde hair was messy and hung slightly in his eyes. He was tall and muscular and even though he looked relaxed, I could feel the excitement rolling off of him as we neared our destination.

I turned to look out the window of the car and all to soon, we pulled up outside of the prison.

I sighed heavily and closed my eyes for a second. I wasn't ready for this. No fucking way was I ready for this.

Braxton was my brothers best friend. He was second in command in the gang, Chase's right hand man. He had been convicted for aggravated assault when he was eighteen and spent three years in jail, then when he was 21, he got out.

I had always had a major thing for him, but I was only young back then, so he obviously didn't want much to do with me. When he got out of jail, I was seventeen and he was a little more interested, being all flirty with me, but even though we had some really hot make out sessions and some steamy moments, nothing ever led to sex.

Then he got sent back to prison for murder, where he had been ever since, but today was the day he got out. He was twenty nine now and I am twenty five.

I chewed on my fingernail, nervous out of my mind, my stomach felt like it was about to make me hurl at anytime and my heart was pounding like a jackhammer. I hadn't seen Braxton in eight years because I was never able to visit him. Chase made it very clear that I wasn't to step foot in the jail, it was to risky because of the MC. We are all criminals and our club was very well known, meaning Chase and I were well known.

Chase climbed out of the car and I followed him after taking a deep breath. I could feel the guys from the other car following along behind me and it made me feel a little better, safer. Chase reached the wall of the prison and leaned against it, pulling out a cigarette and lighting it up, waiting. I stopped with him and shifted my weight on one leg, trying to look un-phased by the entire situation.

"Nice shorts, Parker." Doug, one of the guys in the club snickered as he gripped my wrist, getting close to me.

"Are these men giving you a hard time, ma'am?" A voice asked before I could bite Doug's head off.

I turned towards the voice and froze instantly. A cop was standing there, eyeing me and the group of large brawny men. Braxton stood beside the man, his hands in his jean pockets. Holy shit, he was so hot. His dark hair was messed up and shaggy, his blue eyes playful and surprised as he looked at me. He is still a giant, as tall as Chase, he had always been muscly but now he had completely filled out and stocky was muscle, stubble covered his face and his skin was nicely tanned.

"Always." I muttered, answering the question the cop had asked me.

"Sir, I'm going to have to ask you to step away from the lady." He frowned lightly.

"I'm fine." I narrowed my eyes at the cop and snatched my wrist out of Doug's grip, who laughed but kept his hands to himself.

"Braxton, keep your nose clean." The cop turned to him.

"Of course, boss." He grinned, but it was laced with a threat.

"You better." The officer mumbled.

Braxton just continued to grin at him.

"See ya later, Brax." He sighed and shook his head, walking back inside.

"Let's get the fuck outta here." Chase muttered, on edge. He threw his cigarette on the ground and hugged Braxton, clapping him on the back in a man hug.

"I need a beer." Braxton smiled, hugging him back.

"Let's go." Chase laughed and we all went back to the car. I climbed in the backseat, letting Brax sit up front and I looked down into my lap.

"How was it?" Chase asked when we got on the road.

"Not terrible, you made sure of that." He shrugged.

"Of course." Chase snickered.

"How's business?" Brax leaned back and cracked his neck.

"Great. Parker's more apart of everything now." Chase nodded at me in the back.

"It's good to see you, Park." Brax turned and looked at me.

"I'd be lying if I said the feeling was mutual." I muttered, looking out the window, away from him.

"Parker." Chase growled in warning.

I rolled my eyes and Braxton laughed. They kept talking about mostly business and other events that Brax had missed, then we pulled up outside the bar our MC regulated. We all got out and walked inside together, it wasn't packed, but the place was still busy. We all went straight upstairs to the VIP section and I lounged on one of the couches. Braxton and Chase sat with me on the neighboring couch and a busty waitress walked over, handing the boys a beer each and me a fruity cocktail.

"Can I get a vodka instead?" I eyed the drink, then the woman.

"Of course Miss Greyson." She grinned and scurried off. I rubbed my forehead, needing something stronger. She handed me a raspberry vodka and I gratefully took it and tipped it back, feeling it burn it's way down my throat.

"Thank you." I smiled at her.

"Where's Heidi?" Chase looked at me.

"Dunno, I didn't see her after she went into your room last night." I shrugged.

He nodded and drank his beer. Heidi is my best friend, we had met at a street race when we were eighteen and we had been best friends ever since. She was sleeping with my brother as well, on and off but that didn't phase me.

"Parker, move over." Doug said, coming over to stand in front of me. I lounged into the couch more, making sure my legs stretched out as far as they could. He sighed and lifted me up easily, sitting down and pulling me into his lap.

"Let go of me." I growled, pushing against his chest.

He laughed and held me against him tighter.

"I'd let her go, man." Chase warned.

"She's tiny, I'll be fine." He laughed.

I ran my tongue over my teeth in annoyance and sent my fist into his big stupid nose, making him groan and let go of me, clutching his face. I got off of him and sighed, straightening my outfit.

"Get out before you get blood everywhere." I glared at him.

"Fuckin' hell, Park. You broke my nose." He moaned, standing up, blood streaming down his hand.

"Out." I narrowed my eyes at him and he walked off, going back downstairs.

"Parker, you've not even been here two minutes." The waitress called over, giggling and shaking her head.

I sat back down and looked at my red knuckles.

"You good?" Chase asked lazily.

"Uh huh." I grabbed my drink and gulped the remainder of it down.

Braxton chuckled and shook his head, drinking his beer.

"Brax! Fucking hell brother, you've about doubled in size!" Sin and his twin brother Saint walked in, grinning as they shook Brax's hand and hugged him.

"Could say the same for you two knuckleheads." Brax laughed, tipping back his beer.

Sin and Saint were in the club as well, they had been friends with Brax and Chase since forever. They were identical with their large muscly bodies and striking blue eyes, but where Saint's hair was shaggy and so blonde it was almost white, Sin's was spiky and dyed fire red.

"Good to have you back bro, club hasn't been the same without you." Saint clapped his shoulder.

"Cheers man." Brax nodded.

"We actually organized a present for you." Sin laughed as Chase stood up and grabbed something.

"Welcome back brother." He said, holding up a new leather cut, the clubs name Knight's Of Hell was stitched into the back and Brax's position of VP was on the front.

"Figured the old one wouldn't fit you anymore." Saint laughed.

"Fuck, for real?" Brax grabbed the cut and looked it over, sliding it on over his plain black shirt. "Jesus Christ, that's better." He grinned and pulled Chase into a hug.

"We missed you man." He clapped him on the back

"Parker!" Heidi skipped inside, passed the men and jumped into my lap, holding my shoulders.

"Heidi?!" I raised an eyebrow and laughed.

"Jesse's here." She wagged her eyebrows.

"What?" My smile disappeared.

"Yeah. If you're packing, I'd ditch it." She got to her feet.

"Again? What are you two, dating?" Chase asked with a frown.

"No." I shook my head and stood up, pulling my knife and gun out of my pocket and handing it to Heidi.

"That it?" She checked.

"Yeah." I nodded.

"Okay, well he'll be here in a second." She pushed the knife and gun into her jeans and fluffed up my hair, but I shooed her away, making her pout.

"Whose Jesse?" Braxton asked.

"Some guy that Parker is screwing." Chase growled. "Parker, you can do better."

"I'm not marrying the guy, Chase. And, he's not involved in all this shit so keep your mouth shut." I glared at everyone in the room.

"Yes Parker." The waitresses mumbled, going back to what they were doing. I looked at the guys.

"Fine." Chase sighed and put his hands up.

Braxton put his hands up in surrender as well.

"You've got it, gorgeous." Saint and Sin smiled at the same time.

"Hey Parker." Jesse walked in and I snapped my head around to look at him.

"Damn." Heidi whispered. Jesse was really attractive with his jeans and high vis work shirt and boots on. He was really tall and muscular with a tattoo covering one of his arms. His blonde hair was messy and he had brown puppy dog eyes.

"Hey, what are you doing here?" I asked as he came over to kiss me.

"I just finished work, how was your day?" He smiled and I couldn't help but smile back. He really was the perfect mix of hot and adorable.

"Pretty average." I shrugged one shoulder.

"Hey Chase." He shook my brothers hand.

"Hey man, I'm Jesse." He held his hand out to Braxton and the twins.

"Saint." He shook his hand while Sin started talking to Braxton in a hushed voice.

"Hey Jesse." Heidi smirked in her seductive voice.

"Hey." He smiled at her and walked over to the bar.

"God, where did you find him?" She sighed, staring after him.

"Are you good? Or are you going to rape him the second I turn around?" I laughed at her.

"Shut up." She slapped my arm but kept staring at him. He already had a girl flirting with him at the bar. I sat down and when Heidi still hadn't moved, I sighed and yanked her down with me.

"You're already sleeping with my brother. Get away from him." I rolled my eyes.

"Hey, I'm just sayin' if you ever want a threesome, count me in."

"I'll keep that in mind." I mumbled as he walked back over to me, handing me a new drink.

"Thanks." I smiled and sipped at it.

"So, what do you do?" Braxton asked as all the guys came and sat down with us.

"I work in construction." Jesse looked at Brax and opened his beer, sitting in between me and Heidi. Braxton nodded and looked like he was about to start laughing.

"Parker do you wanna hang out tonight?" Jesse looked at me.

"I have some stuff to do late tonight, I'm sorry." I said evenly.

"Call me when you're done." He shrugged.

"It'll be late and you have work." I sipped my drink again.

"That's cool, just call me." He kissed the side of my head.

"Kay." I nodded.

He stood up and walked to the bathroom.

"Parker's getting laid tonight!" Heidi grinned at me.

"Damn right. Try not to be too jealous." I winked at her and laughed.

"Parker could get laid any night." Sin laughed.

"The benefit of living with a house full of horny men." Saint joined in.

"I think I'd rather scoop my own eyeballs out than sleep with any of the guys." I turned up my lip.

"Any of us?" Sin smirked and his eyes shifted to Braxton for a second, then back to me.

"Yes, any of you. I'm not a club whore." I whipped back at him.

"Damn, okay girl, chill." He raised his hands in surrender.

I looked away and crossed my arms over my chest in annoyance.

"He's going to find out Parker." Chase told me.

"Not if no one says anything.' I looked at him.

"Personally, I don't know how he hasn't heard of you. I mean, you're a Greyson and it's not like he doesn't know you're associated with the Knights." Heidi shrugged.

"He doesn't know my last name to know who I am. And all he knows about the Knight's is that Chase and I are members, no illegal business." I mumbled.

"But still." Heidi pat my thigh.

"I'll break it off soon." I sighed.

"Good." Chase nodded and stood up, grabbing Heidi's hand and pulling her off into another room before she could even say anything.

"Well that's rude." I muttered.

"Chase is a lucky man." Sin mumbled, staring after Heidi.

"You touch her and Chase will kill you. If I don't get to you first." I smiled sweetly.

"Jealous Park?" He smirked again.

"Pfft, why would she settle for the ugly one." Saint laughed.

"You're both like my brothers. Ew." I poked my tongue out and couldn't help but laugh. Even with all the teasing, Saint and Sin saw me as a little sister, Heidi as well. But that didn't stop them from making jokes all the time.

"And everyone knows I'm the hotter one!" Sin turned to his brother.

"In what universe?!" Saint shot back.

"Don't take your shit out of me just because you don't get laid as much as me." Sin grinned.

"You're delusional, shitbrick!" Saint jumped up and Sin stood as well, both of them breaking into a punch up, after a few hits on each other, they just laughed and ended up going back downstairs. Those two fought all the time, but they could never stay mad at each other, they were to close.

"You look really good, Parker." Braxton said, looking at me.

"Yeah, well since last time you saw me, I was seventeen, that doesn't say much." I sighed.

"I missed you while I was in there." His eyes held mine, telling me he was being honest.

I nodded, not knowing how to respond. Of course I missed him too, but I couldn't say that, I couldn't show weakness with him.

"I like that I still make you nervous." He smiled, leaning closer to me.

"I'm not the same girl." I said as sternly as I could, pretending his closer proximity didn't make my heart want to burst out of my chest.

"I can tell. But you'll always have a soft spot for me in your heart, you know that." I ground my teeth together and glared at him. "Stop manipulating me, Braxton. We aren't kids anymore, it won't work." I stood up and looked at him.

"I'm not trying to manipulate you." He frowned.

"Just stay away from me." I sighed and turned to see Jesse coming towards us. "I'm free now?" I raised an eyebrow at him.

"Let's go." He grinned and grabbed my hand, leading me out of the bar, and then outside, into his ute as we drove to his house.

****

Hey guys! Thank you for reading the first chapter of my new book!!

If this is the first time you are reading any of my works, HELLO AND WELCOME!!

Or, if you are checking this out after reading one of my other stories, thank you so much for the love and support <3

What are your thoughts on this first chapter?!

I'd love to know!!

Until next time.. Peace out ;)

- Jade xx

Eight Years Later © Khaotik_Angel , 2016

# Chapter Two:

--------------------------------------------------------

W elcome to the diary of a man that lost his mind so long ago.

- Dear Insanity - Asking Alexandria.

Chapter Two:

Braxton's P.O.V

I watched her walk away with my hand clenched around my beer bottle. She looked amazing in her little denim shorts, white tank top and leather jacket with the clubs patch stitched on it. She was gorgeous. She always had been, but now, she was a woman, a knockout. All grown up. I hated seeing his hand around hers, walking with her. He couldn't protect her, not from rivals. Did she like him? Or was it strictly sex?

I knew I was an idiot for thinking she would still be hung up over me, it had been eight years since I had last seen her.

Did she really think I was trying to manipulate her? I would never do that, not to her. She was the one girl who made me laugh, made me smile. I wasn't just trying to get her into bed back then. Granted, I would of loved to, but I just liked being with her. I loved feeling her mouth of mine, feeling how her heart thumped in her chest as I kissed her. I knew it was wrong of me but I couldn't get away from her, I was drawn to her.

Even today, she was the first person I saw as I stepped outside those prison walls and I almost murdered that Doug guy for touching her, seconds after my release, right in front of a C.O.

The light that radiated from her was blinding. She is so beautiful, so caring, she is unlike any girl I have ever known. I know I'm not good enough for her, but I wanted her. I had honestly hoped that she would be happy to see me and we could pick up where we left off, but I had been an idiot to hope for that.

I tipped the rest of my beer back and relaxed into the couch. She was with him. He was probably kissing her soft lips right now, running his hands along her gorgeous, curvy body, cupping her ass and carrying her to the bedroom.

I clenched my teeth in anger. I hadn't been lying, I had thought of Parker every single day while I was inside. Her smile, and those beautiful bright green eyes that never failed to put me in a trance. At least I still had a piece of her, if she hadn't gotten rid of it. I had tattooed my name on her hip bone one night when we were drunk and she was seventeen. I had always on and off been a tattooist for the gang so I was skilled at it. I remember adding a heart at the end of it and how she giggled as I inked it in, saying it tickled. I hope she still has it. I instinctively rubbed my chest where her name was tattooed over my heart, I had gotten it just before I was jailed, so I never even got a chance to show her.

Jail hadn't been bad, no one ever gave me any grief and Chase had organized for me to get the best cell and, most of the time I didn't even have a cellmate. I was alone a lot which was good, so I could think of Parker at night time when I really missed her. I had spent most of my life wondering what she felt like, how I would feel inside her. Chase also had an arrangement so I was getting laid once every two weeks or so, which I greatly appreciated. He was a good mate.

I looked up as he and the girl, Heidi, made their way back over and sat down.

"Where's Parker?" She asked, looking around.

"She went off with that guy." I mumbled, trying not to let the annoyance leak into my voice.

"Oh, okay." Heidi giggled.

"Chase, I'm going to go. Gotta go see mum." I looked at him.

"Of course man, be careful. Take my car." He handed me his keys. I stood up and walked down and got into his SUV, driving to my mothers house. I took a deep breath and walked up to the door, knocking gently. A little girl opened the door and her eyes widened as she hid herself behind the door.

"Delani, who is it?" My mothers voice called.

"Delani?" I breathed, my eyes going wide.

My mum appeared and she covered her mouth with her hands.

"Braxton." She sobbed, throwing her arms around me, crying into my chest.

"Hey mum." I whispered, hugging her tightly.

"Braxton?" Delani asked, unsure, coming further out.

"Yeah baby, this is Braxton. This is your brother." Mum pulled back slightly so Delani could see me.

"Hey D." I smiled gently, using my nickname for her.

Recognition flickered in her eyes and she grinned, jumping on me. I lifted her and held her to me, hugging her then placing her back down. I walked inside and sat at the table, looking around. The place looked about the same, nothing fancy, but a nice house in general. I had brought her this house when I was eighteen, before I went to jail the first time.

"How are you?" Mum asked, sitting down across from me. Delani sat beside me in the chair.

"I'm good, how are you?"

"I'm doing okay." She nodded, my mum was fairly tall and plump with bright red hair and blue eyes.

"Still working at the diner?" I nodded to her uniform.

"Yeah, just got home." She smiled, looking exhausted.

I nodded and looked down.

"Have you seen Chase?" She asked.

"Yeah, he came and picked me up."

"I'm assuming you will be working for him again?" She raised an eyebrow, looking at my cut.

I nodded.

"Please, be careful, Brax." She reached out and clutched my hand.

"I will." I smiled at her.

"Are you going back to jail?" Delani suddenly asked me, her voice quiet.

I looked at her, surprised, then glanced at mum, who nodded slightly.

"Not if I can help it." I told her honestly.

"I don't want you to go back, Braxton." She shook her head. She would be twelve now, her hair was red like mums, her face was splattered with some freckles and her eyes were big and blue. I hadn't seen my baby sister since she was four.

"Delani, baby, can you let me and Braxton talk?" Mum asked, gently.

She sighed but slowly got up and walked off, down the hall.

"She's so big." I mumbled in shock.

"Yup. She's twelve." Mum nodded.

"I missed you two." I looked at her.

"We missed you too, Brax."

"How's money?" I asked.

She looked down at the table.

"That bad?" I rubbed my forehead.

"I'm lucky to have Chase looking after us." She mumbled.

"I'll help out, I just need some time." I told her.

"No where else will hire me, Brax. I'm working so hard at that diner, I have been for years." Her eyes filled with tears and she buried her face in her hands.

"It's okay mum, I'll help you get back on your feet." I rubbed her arm gently.

"Thank you. You're so good to me." She looked at me with glassy eyes.

"You're my mum." I smiled at her.

"I love you, Brax." She got up and hugged me.

"Love you too." I laughed.

"Look at you, you're a man now." She wiped her eyes and held me at arms length.

"You know what I look like, you came to visit me." I laughed at her.

"I know, I know. I hated seeing you in those cuffs and that uniform. It's good to see you, back to you." She made me bend down so she could kiss my head.

"Yeah, yeah." I pulled back slightly and rolled my eyes.

Mum and Delani were all I had other than the club. My dad had ran out on mum and had been killed before I was even born and Delani's dad had walked out as well. Mum has struggled all her life, she is a good person and a great mother. She was hardly ever home because she was always working but she never complained.

I joined up with Chase and worked out that I was good at that stuff, being a criminal. It meant I could also help out my mum and do something I loved which was great.

Mum didn't really agree with what I was doing but she eventually gave up after I constantly told her I was fine. I brought her the house so we weren't living in a shitty apartment with hookers and pimps running it, I gave her as much as I possibly could until I got arrested and went to prison.

When I got out, I helped her again, but just as she was starting to get back on her feet, I got put away again.

"I'll call you soon, okay? I've gotta get back to the compound." I looked at her.

"Okay honey, I've gotta get some sleep before work again anyway." She smiled and called out for Delani.

"Don't leave!" She pouted.

"I've got to D, I'll see you soon though, okay?" I hugged her.

"Promise?" She held onto me.

"Promise." I smiled and kissed the top of her head.

"Bye." Mum hugged me and I kissed her cheek, going back to the car. I drove back to the familiar mansion and pressed in the code, making the gates swing open. I drove passed some guard and parked the car, walking inside and looking around. It was fancy as fuck still, making me whistle under my breath.

I went straight up to my old room and swung open the door. It was exactly as I had left it. I collapsed on the giant bed and almost moaned it was so good. I kicked off my shoes and looked up at the ceiling.

After a few minutes, I got up and stripped off my clothes, needing a real shower. I let the water wash over me and I closed my eyes in pure bliss. It was little things like this that I missed. Things that people took advantage of, like hot showers, big comfy beds and hot meals that didn't taste like dirt.

I finally stepped out of the shower and wrapped the towel around my waist. I glanced at myself in the mirror and shook my hair out. My body was covered with tattoos, both my arms were full of them, including my hands and they led onto my chest, covering my upper body, back and neck. I had scars spread out everywhere, some from before I went to prison and others from being shanked while I was in the joint.

I looked away and went back to my room, pulling on some underwear, a black long sleeved shirt, some jeans, my cut and work boots. I rolled the sleeves up on the shirt to my elbows and stepped in my wardrobe, finding my safe and cracking it open. I grabbed a wad of cash, my gold Rolex and my weapons, then sat on my bed, cleaning out all my guns and loading them. I clasped my watch on my wrist, shoved the money in my wallet and pushed my handgun in the back of my jeans. My pocket knife slid into my front pocket and I hid my hunting knife on my side, in my jeans. I sighed, relieved to have some protection back and I walked downstairs.

"So is he good in bed?" The girl from before, Heidi, asked.

"He's okay." Parker's laugh carried over to me. I stopped and listened to their conversation.

"What about other stuff?" She pressed.

"He's good."

"But?" Heidi questioned.

"Nothing. It doesn't matter." Parker brushed off.

"Girl."

"He's just so.. Normal." She sighed.

"Elaborate?"

"I'm not used to guys like him. He's so sweet and caring." Parker huffed, out a breath.

"And?" Heidi laughed.

"I don't want sweet and caring. I want danger and excitement." Parker groaned.

I smirked from where I was hidden.

"You always have been a sucker for a bad boy." Heidi giggled.

Parker sighed in annoyance.

"Actually.. You've always had a thing for that bad boy." Heidi said after a second.

"That's in the past. Nothing is happening with me and Braxton." Parker said sternly.

I swallowed the lump in my throat.

"Parker, tell me this. Why did you start seeing Jesse?"

"I dunno. Cause he's hot." Parker said, clearly confused.

"No. Chase told you that Brax was getting out soon and you freaked and threw yourself at the first guy you saw to make yourself stop thinking about him."

"That's the stupidest thing I have ever heard." Parker said defensively.

"Parker-"

"Shut up, Heidi! I don't want to fucking hear it, okay!" She yelled.

"I'm just saying, okay. I'm here for you."

"I fucking hate him. I wish that Chase never met him. I hate that I get nervous every time he looks at me. I hate that I'm glad he's back. I hate that, no matter how hard I've tried to stop thinking about him, I can't. I hate that I still care about him after all he has done to me." Parker rushed out, sadly.

My heart tugged. All I wanted to do was go and hold her in my arms and kiss her all over, telling her how sorry I am.

"Come here." Heidi mumbled. I heard shuffling as they hugged.

"I won't let him hurt me again." Parker said, her voice full of tears.

I heard footsteps and the girls shuffled again, breaking apart.

"What's voice on?" Chase's voice asked.

"Nothing." Parker mumbled.

"Where's Brax?"

"Right here!" I called and walked around the corner, pretending I just got there.

"How's your mum bro?" Chase looked at me.

"Struggling. Thanks for looking after her man." I said sincerely.

"No worries." He smiled.

I snuck a look at Parker. She was leaning against the counter, looking away from me. She was dressed in black jeans, a white tank top that showed her figure and her large chest, and her signature black leather jacket. Her long dark hair was pulled into a high ponytail, bouncing down her back. Fuck, she looked good.

"Let's go make some money." Chase clapped his hands together.

"What are we doing?" I asked.

"Collecting money people owe us and showing you off so word spreads that you're back." Chase looked at me with excitement.

I nodded.

"Parker, go with Brax. You're with me." He winked at Heidi, who giggled.

"Seriously?" Parker groaned.

"Just do it and don't be such a bitch. He just got out of prison, he doesn't need to deal with you icy heart." Chase rolled his eyes and slapped Heidi on the ass, towards the door, then they were gone.

"Follow me." Parker grumbled and walked outside, leading me to a garage. She hopped in a white Range Rover and I climbed in beside her.

Loud music blasted through the custom speakers and she drove in the opposite direction of Chase. She sang along absently and I grabbed the album cover from the centre console.

"The Weeknd?" I frowned.

"God, it's like you were living under a rock." She muttered.

"I know." I looked at the number that was playing to find out the name. "Wicked games?"

"Yup." She popped the p.

It wasn't actually half bad. Not my style, but I still liked it. Parker knew the song word for word, I had forgotten that she was an amazing singer.

'So tell me you love me, only for tonight, only for one night, even though you don't love me. Just tell me you love me, I'll give you what I need. I'll give you all of me. Even though you don't love me.'

I swallowed and looked out the window.

"So when did you get a Range Rover?" I asked as the song finished.

"Chase brought it for me for my eighteenth birthday." She said, absently.

"A white one?" I raised an eyebrow. She was the only one with a white Range Rover, everyone else had a sleek black one, or just rode their Harley's.

"Yeah. I didn't want a black one like everyone else. White's pretty." She caressed the steering wheel.

I nodded in agreement.

"Here we are." She pulled up outside of a strip club.

"We have this side of town, Chase and Heidi have the other." She said, pulling a gun out from inside her jacket. She looked it over, made sure it was loaded and put it back, hopping her perfect ass out of the car. I climbed out as well and we walked to the front door.

"Miss Greyson! Come in." The big bouncer hurried to move the red velvet rope out of the way. He was scared of her. She smirked and walked inside. The scent of beer and cheap perfume hit me like tonne of bricks. Girls were walking around half naked, some of them on poles, while others were rubbing up against men, trying to get them to go with them in the back room. I followed Parker up some stairs and through a door.

"Parker! How are you?!" A woman walked over, hugging her.

"Hey Sophina." She hugged her back.

"So the rumors are true. The infamous Braxton is back." She looked me up and down.

"Of course! Braxton was our best guy, he's loyal to the Knights." She smiled.

I almost fell over with the shock of her being so nice, but then I realized she was just making us all look good, getting my name back out there.

"I know you turn me down every week.. But I've gotta ask, Parker." She looked at Parker, hope in her eyes.

"Sorry Sophina, not interested." She smiled.

"I'd make millions off you alone. You wouldn't even need to have sex with them."

"Still not interested, but thanks."

I swallowed back the ball of anger I had. Parker would never be a stripper. Men ogled over her enough, let alone her being half naked and all over them.

"Come in my office." Sophina sighed and led us into her office. I shut the door behind me and it was now just the three of us.

"You look good, Parker." Sophina casually mentioned, walking over to her safe.

"So do you." Parker ran her hand over the big desk while I hung back.

"Here we are." She handed Parker a wad of cash.

"Pleasure." Parker smiled and turned. Sophina grabbed her wrist and Parker sighed, looking at her.

"You said no to my first offer.. What about my second?" Sophina let her hand slide down so she was holding Parker's hand.

"I'm flattered, but, unfortunately for me, I'm still straight." Parker smiled.

I pursed my lips to stop laughing.

"If you ever switch teams.. Or even feel a little adventurous.. Come see me?"

"Promise." Parker nodded and slipped out of her hand, walking towards me. I opened the door for her and we walked back down and into the car. She leaned over and put the money into an envelope in her glove box. I tried not to focus on her head being so close to my lap.

"So that was interesting." I laughed.

"Shut up, Brax." She grumbled, but laughed as well.

"I think you'd make an adorable couple." I teased her.

"That's cause you're a guy." She rolled her eyes.

"Where to next?" I asked her.

"Some idiot named Hector." She frowned.

We drove to a garage and both climbed out, walking over to it. Parker knocked once, then opened the door.

"Parker! Hey gorgeous." A guy, Hector, I presumed, pulled her into a hug.

"Hector." She hugged him back then looked at him.

"Whose this?" He looked at me.

"This is Braxton. I'm sure you have heard of him. He ran with us about eight years ago." Parker grinned.

I nodded curtly at him.

"The Braxton?" He mumbled, looking at me. A few murmurs came from behind him and I smirked.

"He came back to you after he got out?" Hector said to Parker, but was still watching me.

"Of course. Brax is Chase's best friend. They are practically brothers." Parker laughed.

She was telling the truth, of course. Chase is my brother, he always had been.

"Good to meet you." I mumbled, bored.

"You too." Hector smiled at me.

"Hector, I'm in a hurry." Parker clipped.

"Oh, sure thing babe." He walked over to the desk. "How much?" He looked at her.

"Five grand, Hector. You know that." Parker sighed.

"How about I give you three grand and I take you in the next room. I promise it'll be worth more than two grand." He winked at her.

"Five grand." She repeated.

"I've only got three." He swallowed.

"Well then, I guess we are going into the next room." She cocked her head and his mouth dropped open. I frowned and looked at Parker.

"I'll be back." She looked at me and walked into the other room.

"Holy fuck I can't believe that worked." Hector grinned and followed her inside like a little puppy. The door closed and I leaned against the wall, grinding my teeth together and crossing my arms over my chest. What the fuck was she doing? This isn't the Parker I know.

A scream suddenly broke my train of thought and I snapped my head up, stepping away from the wall. Hector fell out of the room, the force of it knocked the door off it's hinges. He fell on the floor sobbing and Parker calmly walked out, standing over him.

"You better get me that money." She looked at everyone in the room.

"D-Do it!" Hector stammered.

"Aw, was I to rough?" Parker looked down at him with a smirk.

"You're a psycho." He sobbed, clutching his dick that was hanging out.

"That was tame compared to what I'll do to you if you don't get that money." She winked.

"H-Here." A voice said, handing a wad of cash to Parker. She grabbed the money and tossed it to me. I checked it over and looked at her.

"Four." I told her.

"Lying? Really?" She looked at the girl who handed her the money.

"It's all we have!" She cried out.

"Get up." Parker looked down at Hector. He slowly got to his feet, still holding his dick.

"Take a seat." She gestured to a messy desk.

"W-Why?" He looked at her.

"To sort this out of course! I'm a reasonable girl, Hector." She smiled. He walked over to the desk and sat down. Parker looked at me and nodded to him.

I walked over and stood behind him as Parker sat on the edge of the desk beside him.

"How am I going to get that money, Hector?" She asked.

"I'll do anything, Parker." He sobbed.

"Whose that?" She pointed to the girl that lied to her.

"My sister."

"I don't like being lied to, Hector."

"Parker, please."

"Okay, okay. Fine. I won't kill anyone." She rolled her eyes.

"Thank you!" He sniffed loudly.

"Put you hand on the table."

"Why?"

"Put. Your hand. On. The. Table." She glared at him.

He didn't move.

"Brax?" She said, not looking at me.

I grabbed his hand and slammed it on the desk. Parker stood and pulled out her hunting knife.

"What are you doing?!" He screamed.

"Chase and I have been lenient with you before, Hector. We gave you the money. The deal was that you pay back five thousand a week." She said calmly.

"I'm sorry!" He cried.

"You have managed to pay back most of it. You only have this week and next week left." She continued.

"I-I know."

"I'll tell you what. I'll only cut off one of your fingers. It will send a message and I am all about that stuff. I want six thousand next week, Hector."

"You're going to cut off my finger?!" He panicked, struggling in my grip.

"Hold him down." She told me. I placed my other hand on his shoulder, holding him down. Parker raised her knife, bringing it down on his index finger, cutting it clean off. He screamed and I quickly held his mouth to muffle it.

"You bitch!" The sister jumped up and came at Parker with a big knife. I grabbed my gun and shot her in the centre of her forehead, making her fall in a slump.

"No!" Hector screamed.

"See you next week, Hector." She let him go and wiped the blood from her knife on his shirt. She looked at me and we both left, getting back into the car and leaving quickly.

"Are you okay?" I asked her. I'd never seen her like that, Chase hadn't brought her into the club back then.

"I'm fine." She shrugged. "Jesus Christ, we are so fucked up." She laughed.

"What do you mean?" I frowned at her.

"I just tortured him, cut his finger clean off and watched you shoot a girls brains out onto the wall, but I am perfectly fine. I'm thinking about what I want to eat when we're done." She shook her head.

"You're just used to it, Parker. Chase and your dad raised you like a soldier."

"I need to end it with Jesse. I can't bring him into this." She said, mainly to herself.

"You're not a bad person, Parker." I ran my fingers through her ponytail.

"Coming from a con." She laughed and looked at me, parking the car.

"I mean it. You're one of the best people I know." I held her eyes.

"I did miss you." She sighed and looked down.

"You did?" I raised my eyebrows.

"Of course I did. You were my best friend, Brax. Even without all the other feelings I had for you.. You were good to me and I really missed having you around."

"I missed you so much while I was in there." I mumbled.

"Just.. Don't play games with me, okay?" She pleaded.

My eyes snapped up to meet hers.

"I wouldn't." I shook my head with a frown.

"You have before. I was like your own personal toy. You really hurt me." She looked away, embarrassed.

"I hate that I hurt you, Parker. I never wanted to play games with you. I was a mess and I didn't know what I wanted. You were still only seventeen and I was twenty one. It wasn't until I got put in jail again that I realized just how shitty I had been. You deserve better than how I treated you, but I never wanted to hurt you." I told her honestly.

"Let's just get this job done." She muttered, getting out of the car. I followed her and the rest of the night went along smoothly, when we finished up, it was four am.

"I'm hungry." Parker groaned, rubbing her stomach.

"Can we get pizza? I miss pizza." I looked at her.

"Sure." She laughed and drove to a little all hours pizza bar. We walked in together and got a Hawaiian pizza and garlic bread.

"Still your favourite, right?" I looked at her.

"You remember that?" She looked at me in shock.

"Of course." I laughed and we sat down at a table.

"Yes, it's still my favourite." She smiled.

"I also remember coming here with you, Chase and some girl. You were seventeen and some guy grabbed your ass and I beat the shit out of him while Chase made out with the girl."

"Yeah. You threw him into that wall and made a huge hole over there." She laughed at the memory and pointed to the now perfect wall.

"The pizza guys had no idea what to do, they just stared."

"I don't blame them, you're huge, why would they get involved?" She laughed harder.

"You did." I looked at her, sobering up.

"That's because I knew you wouldn't hurt me." She held my gaze.

"You kept trying to rip me off but I didn't listen, saying that the guy should know better than to disrespect you." I mumbled, her eyes entrancing me.

"Until I finally knelt down and looked at you, telling you to stop." Our gaze didn't falter.

"Then I walked outside with you and drove you home, leaving Chase there."

"I cleaned up your hand even though you kept telling me it was fine." She laughed lightly.

"When in reality, it was a bloody mess."

"Most of the blood wasn't yours." She smiled softly.

"Then I walked up to your room and kissed you goodnight." I felt myself stir at the memory of her lips on mine, her body tangled with my own.

"Yeah." She broke eye contact and looked down at the table.

"Memories like that are what helped me when I was inside." I mumbled.

"That pizza is taking awhile." She shifted uncomfortably.

I looked down at the table and we waited in silence until the pizza got there. It tasted incredible, I ate most of it, almost creaming my pants after every bite. Parker drove home, said goodnight and basically ran up the stairs to her room. I sighed and walked slowly up to my own room, having a shower and getting into bed.

****

What do you guys think of Braxton and Parker?!

What about the situation with Hector? What do you think about how Parker handled it?

I would like to dedicate this chapter to one of my best friends on Wattpad. Jess, is an incredible writer and I love her to bits! She is probably my personal favourite Wattpad writer and ALL of her books are in my favourite list, that's how amazing they are! Please, go check her out and give her some support!

Thank you so much for reading! If you enjoyed, hit up that vote button! I loveeee reading comments from you guys and I am very approachable and nice, so feel free to message me anytime!

Until next time..

- Jade xx

Eight Years Later © Khaotik_Angel, 2016

# Chapter Three:

----------------------------------------------------------------

W ell, I've got thick skin and an elastic heart, but your blade - it might be too sharp.

- Elastic Heart - Sia.

Chapter Three:

Parker's P.O.V

I rolled out of bed and ran myself a shower. I wrapped myself in a towel and got changed into a black underwear set, a pair of denim mini shorts and a red plaid shirt with a knot tied in the front, showing my toned flat stomach and the dream catcher tattoo I have that took up my entire side. I have one other tattoo that sits low on my hipbone so it can't be seen unless I'm just in my underwear, it was done to me when I was seventeen, by Braxton when we were both drunk. He is a good tattooist, so it does look good and isn't a total mess, it is simple and is just of his name with a heart at the end. I honestly don't even know if he remembers it now.

I blow dried my hair and let it to hang loosely around my waist. My figure is very curvy, with a small waistline and my skin is tanned. I applied some light makeup and my bright green eyes stood out against my tan skin and glossy black hair. Pushing my gun in the back waistband of my shorts out of habit, I walked downstairs.

"Braxton told me what happened last night." Chase said from the table, with Braxton beside him and Heidi in the kitchen wearing one of Chase's button up shirts and nothing else.

"Yeah. Should be sorted out by next week." I told him, opening the fridge.

"Did you leave us for Sophina this week?" Heidi laughed, wagging her eyebrows.

"Shut up." I laughed at her.

"Just for that, I'm not making you food." She poked her tongue out.

"What are you making?" I stood on my tip toes and the smell of bacon and eggs filled my nose. I pouted at her.

"Don't give me that face! Ugh, fine, okay miss spoilt." She sighed.

"I'm not spoilt!" I gasped.

"Please, you have everyone wrapped around your pretty little finger." Chase chuckled.

"You included." I smirked at him.

He shook his head and smiled.

I laughed and skipped over to make a coffee.

"Hey boss. Brax." Doug walked in wearing a pair of jeans and nothing else, his abs and tattoos on full display.

"Best part about working here, is that all the guys are built so damn well. So many hot guys to perv on." Heidi whispered to me.

I laughed and shook my head at her.

"Hey Heidi, hey Park." Doug turned to us, his eyes lingering us both.

"Hey Douglas, how's the nose?" I said sweetly, pouring two cups of coffee and handing him one.

"Had worse." He shrugged, taking the cup from me.

"Well you look like hell." I smiled. His nose was swollen and his eyes were black and blue. Even I had to admit he was still good looking though.

"You and I both know that's a lie." He winked at me.

"I'm sorry, did you just wink? It's hard to tell when your eyes are swollen almost shut." I sipped my coffee.

"One of these days, girl, I swear to God-" He said in a husky voice.

"What? You swear what?" I pressed, raising an eyebrow.

"Yeah Doug, you swear what?" Chase cut in, his eyes staring daggers at him. Braxton was glaring at the table, his hand gripping his coffee mug so tight, I wouldn't be surprised if it shattered to pieces.

"Nothing Sir. Sorry." Doug cleared his throat and shifted his weight.

"So manly, Doug." I laughed and continued drinking my coffee.

He shot a glare at me.

"Parker! Your little toy boy is here for you!" One of the guys yelled across the house.

"Who?!" I frowned in confusion.

"Hey gorgeous." Jesse rounded the corner, looking pissed off, I'm assuming from the nickname.

"Jesse? What the fuck are you doing here?" My eyes bugged.

"You left this at my place? Uh, I'm sorry?" He held up my purse.

"Oh. Thank you." I said a little quieter. The gun in my shorts was suddenly burning into my skin. Fuck. I looked at Doug for help. He looked down and smiled smugly. He reached down and grabbed my ass so Jesse couldn't see, then he turned and walked away. I clenched my jaw and glared after him.

"Work got cancelled today so I figured I'd bring it to you. I checked your license to see where you lived." Jesse continued, looking around, clearly intimidated by the huge mansion.

"That's really sweet, thank you." I smiled and looked at Heidi for help. She pointed to her outfit or there, lack of, with a stupid expression. Of course. She couldn't help me.

"What are you doing?" Jesse laughed at me, standing stock still.

"Nothing." I smiled and looked at him.

He pulled me in for a hug, but I quickly grabbed his hands and held them at my hips, kissing him quickly.

"Are you okay?" He frowned down at me.

"I'm fine!" I smiled and pushed my hair out of my face.

"Hey man." Braxton said from beside me, holding his hand out to Jesse.

"Hey... Uh, sorry man, what was your name again?" Jesse frowned, thinking.

"Brax." He smiled.

"Brax.." Jesse continued to frown, testing the name. Shit. He would piece it together in a second, I had always told him that Braxton was just an old boyfriend, and I had stupidly gotten his name tattooed on my body. In truth, I didn't regret it at all. Braxton was a huge part of me, as much as I would deny that to everyone.

"So are you and Parker dating? She's a.. Good friend of mine." Brax casually draped his arm around my waist and leaned back against the counter.

Jesse looked at me and sighed slightly, "We're just friends." His voice leaked of disappointment.

"Okay well, you better look after my girl." He put an emphasis on my and slowly ran his hand down my bare back, making my breath speed up. His fingers were leaving trails of electricity along my skin, just like they always had. I shuddered slightly and bit the inside of my cheek.

"Are you cold?" Jesse cocked his head to the side, noticing.

"I'm fine." I smiled. Braxton's hand gripped the gun and he pulled it out of my shorts, holding it against my behind.

"Hey Jesse!" Heidi quickly grabbed his attention.

He looked at her and Braxton quickly pushed the gun in his jeans, looking at me, his eyes burning, like he had felt the electricity as well.

"Hey Heidi." Jesse started talking to her.

"Thank you." I whispered.

"Anytime Princess." Braxton smiled a sexy half smile and walked back over to sit by Chase.

Princess.

That is what he always used to call me.

The way he said it made me swallow a lump of emotion that had formed in my throat. I grabbed my coffee and sipped it, trying to dislodge the tennis ball in my throat. I casually went over to the table and sat down, acting like my world hadn't just stopped.

"Thanks for all the help." I grumbled to Chase.

"You're a big girl." He muttered, staring at Heidi, still in his shirt. His jaw clenching and unclenching.

"Are you jealous, Chasey?" I grinned and my eyes widened at him. Braxton chuckled quietly.

He froze and extremely slowly turned his head to glare at me, like he wanted to literally murder me.

"You are!" I whisper yelled, not intimidated in the least.

"Why would I be jealous?" He said in a hard voice.

"You like Heidi." I smiled.

"I'm Chase fucking Greyson. I have women falling over me, why would I settle for one?" He asked like I was an idiot.

"Then why are you only fucking one?" I said evenly and met his eyes.

Chase's eyes flashed and he was about to probably knife me, but Heidi and Jesse sat back at the table, breaking up the conversation. Jesse sat beside me and kissed my head, placing his hand on my thigh. Heidi set down a huge plate of food and a stack of plates.

"Dig in." She smiled, sitting at Chase's side.

"Do you all live here?" Jesse asked, grabbing some bacon.

"I come and go." Heidi shrugged.

"A lot of people live here." I told him, spearing an egg and popping it in my mouth.

"So it's for the Knights?" He mumbled.

"Something like that." Chase shrugged.

Jesse nodded and frowned slightly.

"Do you wanna do something today?" He asked.

"Actually, Parker's busy with me today." Heidi interjected, lying through her teeth, we had no plans today.

"Oh, what are you guys up to?"

"Who knows what the day will bring." She giggled.

"Okay, well call me later or something?" He looked at me.

"Kay." I smiled at him.

"I'll go." He stood up and stretched, making his shirt ride up, exposing his tanned abs. Heidi choked on her food as she ogled him.

"You okay?" He asked her, a little concerned.

"I'm good." She giggled.

"Okay.." He pulled me to my feet and kissed me quickly before he left.

"Jesse!" Heidi called out.

He turned to her, an eyebrow raised.

"Can you get me a glass of water?" She asked.

I bit back a laugh.

"Uh, sure." He walked into the kitchen.

"Glasses are at the very top." She informed him.

He reached up and opened the cupboard, showing more of his defined abs and back. He grabbed a glass, filled it with water and set it in front of Heidi.

"Thanks." She purred.

"All good. See ya." He kissed me again and left.

"So subtle." I looked at my best friend.

"I have a weakness for abs okay. Chase knows this." She looked at him.

"Ugh." I scrunched up my nose and sat back down.

"But seriously.. How do you reject a guy like that? He's so fucking hot. If I were you, I'd spend all day either licking his abs or letting him have his way with me." Heidi laughed.

"We've spoken about this." I looked at her, making her remember our conversation last night.

"Danger shmanger." She mumbled.

"What?" Chase frowned.

"Nothing." I muttered.

"He's not that good looking." Chase shrugged.

"Are you crazy? I mean, you're way hotter. But he is fine." Heidi ran her hand down Chase's bicep. He grinned at her.

"Plus, from what I've heard, you're better in bed." She continued.

"Dude." I glared at her.

She ignored me and Chase kissed her deeply.

I looked away and pushed my plate to the side, turned off any food. Braxton was sitting there, arms crossed, staring at the ceiling, seemingly in his own world.

He looked hot as hell in his jeans, black jumper and leather cut on. I can tell he has a better body than Jesse does. Jesse is thin and muscly, whereas Brax is stocky, his arms were bigger and his chest is broader. God, he was so sexy. I wonder what he looks like with his shirt off these days? He has always had a great body, but now he has filled out more, become even manlier. I bit my lip gently, thinking about it, then snapped out of it. No, no, no. I couldn't fall for him again. I looked away and huffed out a breath.

Chase grabbed Heidi and pulled her upstairs to his room, leaving me alone with Braxton.

"Wanna go for a drive?" He asked me.

"Why?" I raised an eyebrow.

"Because I miss driving. I haven't done it in eight years. Plus, I've got some stuff to do." He shrugged.

"Okay." I took the plates to the sink and filled it with hot soapy water. I started washing and Braxton grabbed a towel, drying them and putting them away.

"Bet it was good to sleep in your own bed again." I said, absently.

"You have no idea." He laughed once.

"We made a good team last night."

"Yeah, we did." He smiled at me, his blue eyes shinning.

"Don't do that." I looked down into the water.

"Do what?" He asked in confusion.

"The eye thing." I muttered.

"Eye thing?" He frowned.

"The eye thing you do." I sighed and let out the water, then walked up to my room. I brushed though my hair quickly and when I turned around, Braxton was lying on my bed, his hands behind his head as he stared at the ceiling.

"Jeez Brax." I put a hand over my heart.

"Sorry." He mumbled sadly.

"What?" I walked over to the bed and looked at him.

"I'm not trying to manipulate you." His deep voice was so sad and quiet.

"I need my gun." I said stupidly.

He stood up and looked at me, like he was fighting with himself. He blew out a huge breath and reached back, handing me my gun. I pushed it in my shorts and then walked out the room, going downstairs. I was afraid if I stood in the room for any longer with him, I'd shove him on my bed and tear his clothes off.

"You wanna take your car to the warehouse?" He asked, coming down the stairs.

"I'll take another car there and get one of the others to pick it up." I turned to look at him.

"Okay." He nodded.

I grabbed a set of keys and we walked outside, getting into a black SUV. Brax climbed in and I drove to the warehouse across town where Braxton had stored his car. When we pulled up, we got out and Braxton grabbed his keys, unlocking the garage door and pulling it up.

"Hey gorgeous." He muttered, touching the car cover.

I rolled my eyes.

He gently pulled the cover off the car and set it on the floor.

"I missed you baby." He continued, running his hand over the flawless sleek black paint job and grinned.

The car was amazing, I still remember when he got it. He had brought it and restored the entire thing. It was a 67' Impala that he adored. He didn't want a Range Rover, he had this, his dream car, his baby. He had a Harley he loved as well, but his Impala held a special place in his heart.

Braxton climbed in the car and ran his hand over the interior with the biggest smile on his face.

"Coming?" He called.

"No, but I'm assuming you are." I muttered as I climbed in. He looked at me with a smirk and I looked away from him. Leaning over me, he grabbed an envelope from the glove box, opening it and looking at the contents inside.

"Where to first?" He asked.

"Where ever your heart desires." I laughed.

He nodded and started the car. The engine roared to life and Brax audibly moaned at the sound, letting his head roll back. It sounded amazing, both the car and him. Brax was really good with cars, or basically anything with an engine. It was his passion.

The engine idled loudly, the sound was chunky and powerful with a promise of menace. Braxton ran his hands over the wheel and slowly, we left the warehouse. He got out and closed up the garage, then got back in and we peeled out of the lot. He was slow at first, letting the car warm up, then he flattened it and started weaving around other cars. The view was going passed in a blur, the engine roared, like it was thrilled to have Braxton back. It attracted a lot of attention, almost everyone turned their head as they saw us. I saw some men almost cream their pants at the sight and I rolled my eyes with a smile.

"You okay? Not scared or anything?" He glanced at me quickly.

"Brax, I've been driving with you for ages, I trust you, you're a good driver." I snuck a smile at him.

He chuckled and put his foot down further. It was true, Braxton is an incredible driver, he was a star at the street races we used to attend.

He turned down a road, making the cars back end flick out gracefully, then he brought it back in, driving up into the hills. He handled the car so easily, like they were connected. He was so relaxed and clearly more than happy to be driving his car again. When we reached the top of the hills, Braxton went down a little dirt path that wasn't even a road and he weaved around for awhile before stopping and getting out of the car. I got out as well and followed him to where he was standing.

"You realize the lookout is back there, right?" I frowned, looking at my feet to make sure I didn't fall as I reached him.

"You don't remember this place?" He sounded surprised and a little sad.

"What do you mean?" I asked.

"Look." He whispered.

I looked up at him in confusion.

"Not at me, you idiot." He chuckled and pointed out. I followed his finger and gasped. You could see the entire city from here. It looked so beautiful, much better than the lookout everyone else went to.

Brax and I had come here a lot when I was seventeen. In this very car. He told me that he loved it here and often came here to think. He made me promise that I would never show anyone, that it would be our thing. He said that he had never showed anyone before. We used to come here at night a lot, sometimes he dragged me out of bed and drove me here so we could just watch the sunrise together. This had also been our favourite make out spot, mainly in or on the car.

"I haven't been here in years." I mumbled, still looking at the beautiful view.

"So you do remember?" He sounded a little nervous, which is very un-Braxton.

"Of course." I frowned slightly, how could I not of clicked when we drove up here.

"I'm glad my first time back is with you." I felt his hand on the small of my back and it sent shocks through my system.

"The last time I came here was when you were sentenced. I came here and cried for hours. I haven't been back since." I whispered, feeling tears sting my eyes. I felt Braxton move so he was behind me and he wrapped his arms around my bare waist, leaning back against the hood of the car as we looked out at the view.

"Did you tell anyone about this place?" His breath tickled my ear.

"No." I shook my head lightly.

"Good." His arms tightened around me.

"I can't believe we are here, all these years later." I laughed once.

"I always said that when I get out, I want to bring you back here." His voice was deep and husky. I turned in his arms slowly and he didn't move an inch. He watched me carefully, his arms still around me. I placed my hands on his sides and looked up at him. Slowly, Braxton bent down so I could pull away if I wanted too, then he kissed me.

As soon as our lips touched, it sent jolts through my entire body, I kissed him back and ran my hands up his hard abs and chest, wrapping them around his neck. I played with his hair, pulling gently and he moaned into my mouth, deepening the kiss and running one of his hands up into my hair while the other held me to him by the small of my back. His tongue traced my lower lip, asking for entrance. I opened my mouth and his tongue stroked mine, our mouths moving together expertly, we already knew each others lips and bodies so well.

I melted into his chest, leaning into him more and he held me up, not breaking the kiss. I felt like I was on fire. A good fire. He sent tingles through my entire body everywhere he touched me and I knew I was effecting him just as much. I was standing in between his legs, where he was leaning against the car, so I didn't have to reach up as much as I usually would and I could also feel him digging into me, hard and throbbing. I resisted the urge to push against him and tried to ignore it, which was damn near impossible.

Even with the excitement in his pants, he was gentle and sweet with me, caressing me and holding me to him. He didn't try to deepen the kiss any further, making it overly sexual, he just kissed me lovingly. After a few minutes, I pulled back slightly and he stopped instantly. I moved so my arms were around him and I snuggled into his chest, breathing in his manly scent. God, he always smelt so good. Ever since I first met him, to now at twenty nine, he smelt the same. It was an incredible smell and it made me feel safe. I closed my eyes and felt myself physically relax into him. He held me to him, running his other hand through my hair with his chin resting gently on my head.

"God, I missed you so much, Princess, you have no idea." He whispered, holding me tighter.

"I missed you." I breathed, squeezing my eyes closed when I felt the tears prickle there. It was true, I missed him so much. I just wasn't sure I could trust him a hundred percent yet.

"Do you wanna go?" I asked quietly.

"If you want.." He trailed off.

I nodded and pulled back off of him.

"Your eyes are glassy." He stroked my cheek gently, looking concerned. I stepped back, making his hand fall to his side and I forced a small smile, walking back over to the car and getting in. I watched him sigh and come over, getting in and starting the car. He pulled out and drove along the road, fiddling with the stereo until suddenly Come on feel the noise by Quiet Riot came on. Brax laughed and turned it up loud, not having heard his music for years. Braxton was always into all kinds of music, but he especially loved music from the seventies and eighties.

"Come on feel the noise! Girl's, rock your boys!" He sang loudly.

"We'll get wild, wild, wild. Wild! Wild! Wild!" I continued.

"So you think I got an evil mind, I tell you honey! I don't know why! I don't know why!" He laughed with a glint in his eye.

I laughed loudly and he turned to smirk at me, placing his hand on my thigh. I'm honestly not even sure he realized he did it, it was just a habit, for us both, so I let him be.

The song finished and we listened to some more music like Led Zeppelin and The Rolling Stones.

We pulled up outside a house and Brax turned the car off.

"Where are we?" I asked him.

"My mums. Come on." He smiled and climbed out of the car.

"I've never met your mum." I stated as I pushed my gun under the seat and got out of the car.

"She works a lot." He shrugged and we walked up to the door. He knocked and after a few seconds, a girl answered the door.

"Braxton!" She squealed and jumped on him. He laughed and held her in his arms, walking inside.

"Hey kiddo, where's mum?" He asked.

"She's in the shower, she just woke up." She smiled at him.

"Okay well we will wait for her." He put her down gently. "Delani, this is my friend, Parker. Parker, this is my little sister, Delani." He ruffled her hair.

"Hi Delani." I smiled at her.

"Hi." She blushed, shy.

"Don't be shy, D. It's okay."

"I'm much nicer than him." I laughed.

She laughed and looked at me properly.

"Wow, you're beautiful." Her eyebrows rose.

"Not as pretty as you." I winked.

She laughed and gave me a quick hug.

"Braxton?" A woman's voice asked.

"Hey mum." He smiled at her.

She ran over to him and hugged him tightly.

"You okay?" He frowned and hugged her back, on alert.

"I'm fine. I just know that I didn't imagine you yesterday now." She pulled back and looked up at him.

"This is my friend, Parker. Park, this is my mum, Adena." He gestured to me.

"Parker Greyson?" She looked at me with wide eyes.

"Yes ma'am." I smiled and held my hand out to her.

"I-It's so nice to meet you. Thank you so much for all you and your brother have done!" She hugged me and I chuckled, hugging her back. Her hugs were so warm and comforting.

"No problems." I said into her red hair.

"Come, sit down." She ushered us to the table.

I sat down and Braxton sat beside me with Delani across from me, picking up the book she had been reading.

"What are you reading?" I asked her.

"A werewolf story." She smiled at me.

"Like Twlight or something?" I cocked my head.

"No!" She wrinkled up her nose. "This one is just werewolves, no vampires."

"So what happens?" I smiled at her.

"A girl meets her mate at a funeral and he turns out to be a really powerful Alpha of a pack and she needs to help him run it, but she's only half blooded." Delani gushed.

"Sounds interesting." I laughed.

"Here." Braxton handed his mum an envelope. She peaked inside and then looked at him, her eyes tearing up.

"It's all I've got at the moment. I'll get more when I start doing more jobs." He told her.

"Thank you, Braxton." She hugged him again.

"Don't worry about it." He laughed lightly.

"Let me make lunch for you two. What would you like?" She smiled at us both.

"Whatever." He shrugged and she hurried off into the kitchen.

Braxton stood up and I followed him as he walked down the hall and into a room. It was simple, with a cupboard that only had one door on it and a big bed that looked like it hadn't been slept in in years. Then I realized, it hadn't. This was Braxton's room.

He looked around and chuckled, touching the cupboard. I walked in and sat on the bed, leaning against the headboard.

"Your mum is really sweet." I smiled.

"She is. She deserves better than all this." He mumbled, going through his things.

"You're so good to her." I watched him with a small smile on my face.

"She's my mum." He shrugged and pulled out a backpack, putting it on the bed. he sifted through it and pulled out some guns and knives.

"When is the last time you lived here?" I waved my hand around.

"Probably not since I was about eighteen. I was living here when I got arrested the first time. But when I got out, I lived with you and Chase, before I went back." He shrugged.

"So, if I look under your bed, I'd probably find a stack of dirty magazines?" I teased.

He bent down and felt under his bed and laughed. "Yup." He stood back up and kept going through the bag.

"Typical." I laughed and rolled my eyes.

"I was eighteen." He smirked at me.

"You had girls throwing themselves at you, so you really didn't need them." I pointed below the bed.

"I didn't just sleep around with any girl who offered." He frowned lightly.

"How old were you when you lost your virginity?" I cocked my head to the side, curious.

"Why?" He looked at me, confused and amused.

"Curious." I shrugged.

"About fifteen." He rolled his eyes.

"Who to?" I laughed.

"Her name was Anna. She was eighteen and my neighbour at the time." He chuckled at the memory.

I nodded.

"You?" He looked at me.

"Me what?" I stared at the ceiling.

"Oh come on! I told you!." He laughed.

"Fine." I huffed out a breath. "I was seventeen and it was at a party." I rolled my eyes.

"Seventeen?" He asked quietly.

"Yeah." I looked down.

"Was it while I was out? Or when I went back to jail?" He asked, his voice strained.

"A couple months after you went back."

"Who to?"

I looked away.

"Do I know him?"

I nodded.

"Parker, who?" He pressed.

"Digger.." I mumbled.

"Digger?' He repeated.

"That's why he isn't in the club anymore. I got really drunk and he led me away and said he would help get me to bed so I was safe. He asked me if I missed you and I said yes and he told me he would take my mind off it. Then it just kinda happened. Chase came in and saw him on top of me and flipped out. He beat the shit out of him and I that was the last time I saw him." I said, not looking at him.

"Digger was my mate.. He knew what you meant to me. What a fucking dick. He's lucky I wasn't there. I would of killed him." He said absently as rage filled his eyes.

"It wasn't just him. I went along with it." I shrugged, ashamed.

"You were drunk. He better prey I never run into him or I'll end up going away for life." He clenched his jaw.

"I wish I lost it to you, to be honest." I blurted out, then smacked a hand on my mouth, my eyes bugging.

"Why?" He asked me, completely shocked as he sat on the bed beside me.

"Can you just ignore I said that?" I groaned, covering my face.

"No." He said quietly.

"I dunno! Cause I've always cared about you. It would of meant something, even if it didn't for you." I sighed.

"You don't think it would mean anything to me?" He asked.

I shrugged.

"I've wanted to sleep with you forever but I would never push you. You were, and are, the only girl I have ever cared about." He muttered.

"You would of made it more special for me. And you wouldn't of been so rough with me." I hugged my knees.

"C'mere baby girl." He pulled me into his lap and hugged me tightly. "I'm so sorry." He sighed, kissing the top of my head.

"What for?" I asked into his chest.

"If I didn't get put away, I would've been here the whole time. I wouldn't of let Digger, or anyone else touch you. You would be mine." He mumbled.

"It's not your fault, Brax." I shook my head.

"I wish I was the one who took your virginity as well." He sighed. "But not just to sleep with you. But because you are right, I would of made it special for you and I would of been gentle with you so you could at least enjoy it." He continued.

The thought of that made me squirm a little with want.

"You okay?" He asked, noticing.

I nodded and bit my lip. I rolled suddenly so I was straddling him and his hands instantly went to my hips, his face filled with confusion and surprise. I leaned in and kissed him hard. He moaned a little in surprise and kissed me back.

I felt him harden beneath me and my breath hitched in my throat, feeling him right there. I unconsciously started grinding myself against him and he groaned, clutching my hips tighter. I bit his lower lip and his tongue mixed with mine, hungrily.

Braxton suddenly flipped us over so he was hovering over me and he dipped his head, kissing my neck. My legs spread wide and he was between them, holding himself up effortlessly. I wrapped my legs around his hips and he growled as I ground against him, running his hands up and down my sides.

I could feel how much dampness was between my thighs and I whimpered, needing him. He chuckled and kissed down to my chest, pushing my top to the side. He moved my bra and then his hot tongue was running over my nipple, making me arch my back and moan.

"Brax? Mum said lunch is ready!" Delani called, knocking on the door.

He sighed in anger and I giggled.

"Okay!" I called out.

Braxton pulled up and looked at me, his eyes full of lust, almost making me melt into a puddle on the bed.

"Sorry." I smirked and kissed his jaw, pushing him off me.

"I feel like a fucking teenager again. Foolin' around without my mum finding out." He grumbled.

"You'll live." I stood and straightened my outfit.

"Easy for you to say. You're not the one with blue balls." He grunted.

Aw, poor baby." I leaned over and kissed him once more.

"You're such a tease." He groaned and stood up.

I couldn't help but look at the giant bulge in his jeans. It was huge. And that was with jeans containing it. I had forgotten just how big he was.

"Careful babe, keep looking at me like that and I'll throw you back on the bed." He smirked.

"It's a good thing we didn't go any further, cause by the looks of it, you would rip me in half." I muttered.

He walked over to me and kissed me deeply. "You'd love it. Once you adjusted to my size, you'd have the time of your fucking life." He mumbled sexily.

I moaned at his words. Literally moaned.

"Let's go eat." He chuckled.

I slapped his chest and walked out of the room, going to the table and sitting down.

"I just threw a lasagne in the oven." Adena set down a big oven dish filled with lasagne and Delani set out plates and forks.

"Looks great." I smiled at her. She served everyone up a piece and we sat and ate in mostly silence. Well, we ate, Braxton basically inhaled his first and second helping and was now on his third, eating it at a more humane speed.

"This alone is why I'm staying out. The food!" He moaned.

Everyone laughed and I helped Adena clear the table.

"Oh, I'll do that, Parker." She smiled at me.

"Don't be silly." I laughed and insisted on washing the dishes while Braxton dried and put them away.

"I'll see you later." Braxton hugged his mother as we got ready to leave.

She nodded and squeezed him, her eyes closed tightly. She pulled away and Delani hugged him as well.

"Nice meeting you." I smiled and Adena pulled me into a hug.

"You come around whenever you want, you hear me?" She told me, smoothing my hair out.

I nodded and hugged Delani, then left with Brax. We climbed in the car and I grabbed my gun from under the seat, holding onto it. Braxton drove back to the mansion and he parked the car, walking inside with me.

"Club tonight?" Heidi grinned as soon as I stepped inside.

"Uh, sure." I shrugged.

"Yay! I'll tell Chase!" She clapped, jumping up and down.

"Chase is coming?" I groaned.

"Why?" She cocked her head in confusion.

"I don't wanna third wheel while you guys grind all over each other!" I complained.

"I promise to party and be a crazy single girl with you." She raised her right hand in a pledge.

"Then why is Chase coming?" I chuckled.

"Cause you know we are going to be the best looking girls in that place and he can scare off all the guys who aren't hot." She winked.

I laughed and shook my head at her.

"I'll come." Braxton shrugged.

"See, now we have a body guard each." Heidi bumped my shoulder.

"Like we couldn't look after ourselves." I scoffed.

"I plan to look good and not ruin my look with someone else's blood." She raised an eyebrow.

"Good point." I grinned at her. "God, I haven't drank in so long."

"That's because you have been crazy obsessed with work. Let loose girl. Go make out with a thousand guys and shake that fine ass of yours." Heidi shimmied her hips and I burst out laughing.

"Don't encourage her. I'll shoot anyone who looks at my baby sister like a piece of meat." Chase grumbled, rounding the corner.

"Chase let her be. We're much tamer than we were when we were teenagers!" Heidi laughed.

"Thank fuck for that! I lost count of the amount of times I had to bail you both out of jail, or got into fights because of your antics." He glared at us both.

Braxton laughed and I blew Chase a kiss.

"I could've used your help back then, these two were wild." Chase looked at Brax, then shook his head.

"Were? Ugh, see Park! We need to let loose!" She complained.

"Then let's do it." I grinned at her mischievously.

"Oh, hell no." Chase looked at us.

"Yay!" Heidi jumped on me and hugged me tightly.

"Fuck." Chase muttered, but laughed.

"Let's get ready!" Heidi grabbed my hand and ran upstairs, dragging me along with her.

I got undressed and stood in my underwear, looking through my clothes. I pulled on a pair of tight black leather high waisted shorts and a white crop top with my signature leather jacket. I pulled on some black high heeled combat boots and walked into the bathroom. I re-applied my makeup, making my eyes more dramatic and adding a plum lip colour. My hair hung loose and I pushed it to the side, fluffing it up and grabbing my hunting knife, hiding it inside my jacket. With one more look in the mirror, I walked downstairs where Heidi was waiting with the guys.

"Woo! Damn girl!" Heidi shouted.

I laughed and did my best model pose, spinning in a circle.

"You're both going to make me murder someone tonight." Chase clawed his face.

"I won't, but this booty might." Heidi winked at him.

Heidi has mocha coloured skin, she is thin but has some serious killer curves. She doesn't have much in the boob area, but her booty makes up for it. Her hair was black and fuzzy, like an afro, it was always flawless and bouncy, in tight ringlet curls. Heidi wore light blue jeans, a white crop top and black heels, with big golden hoops in her ears.

"Girl gotta booty like pow." I said as I stopped beside her.

"Mmhmm." She wiggled her hips and I laughed loudly.

Brax had changed out of his jumper and was now wearing a black shirt and black leather cut, I tried to pretend not to notice that his eyes were roaming over my body.

"Let's go." Chase sighed and we all made our way out to the Range Rover, climbing in, going to the club.

As soon as the bouncer saw Chase, he stumbled to let us through without waiting in line. I smiled at the bouncer and shot him a wink, making his eyes pop out of his head.

"Let's do shots!' Heidi jumped up and down.

"I'm in." I smiled.

That was how it started, just a few harmless shots.

I don't know exactly how it escalated from there, but now there was a crowd around us as we raced each other in a line of shots, trying to reach the middle first. Heidi grabbed the last shot glass and I quickly placed my mouth over it, jerking her arm so she tipped it down my throat.

"You dirty little cheater!" She gasped as everyone laughed.

I winked at her and she broke into a fit of laughter.

"Next game?" The bartender smirked.

"Yes!" Heidi clapped her hands.

"Sure thing girls, what now?" He chuckled.

"I've got it." Heidi's eyes twinkled with mischief. She got on her tip toes and whispered something in the bartenders ear. He laughed loudly, tipping back his head.

"What have you done?" I looked at her.

She winked and the barman lifted a girl onto the bar, making her lie on her back.

"You didn't." I laughed and looked at Heidi.

"Oh, but I did." She grinned wickedly.

"Jesus Christ." Chase laughed from where he and Braxton were standing, right behind me.

"Time to make everyone question our sexuality." Heidi laughed, going over to the girl. She did the routine of tequila, salt and lime, making all the jaws drop in the process, then looked at me.

"That's all you got?" I scoffed, all the alcohol settling in and giving me an overload of confidence.

"Off you go then, prove that you aren't boring." She giggled.

I raised an eyebrow at her. "Boring? Bitch please, I've already won."

"I dunno, that was pretty hot." The barman looked at me as he set up a shot of tequila between the girls breasts, a line of salt going up her stomach and a lime resting on her mouth. I hoisted myself on the bar and straddled the girl, which got everyone very interested.

"Fuck. You've got me." Heidi laughed, shaking her head.

My eyes connected with Braxton's, above Heidi's head. He was watching me intently, his eyes dark with lust.

I giggled and got back to the task at hand. I slowly placed my hands on either side of the girls body and bent down, running my tongue along the line of salt, slowly, then I grabbed the shot glass in my mouth and tipped it back. I spat the glass out into the barman's open hand and then bent down, grabbing the lime out of her mouth and biting into it. I spat out the wedge and hopped off the girl easily. I was deafened by laughs, cheers and snide comments.

I looked at Heidi.

"I forgot how competitive you are. You'll do anything to win." She laughed.

I poked my tongue out at her and we walked up to the VIP section, away from the leering men.

"I like careless you." Heidi giggled. "You're so much fun! This is the Parker I love! The flirty, sassy, sexy little minx who lived for dancing and drinking!"

"I haven't missed it." Chase grumbled. "By the way, I really didn't need to see that whole show, Park." He turned up his lip.

"Aw Chasey, I'm still your baby sister!" Slurring, I jumped on him, knowing he would catch me.

He chuckled and held me to him, hugging me, then he gently placed me back on my feet.

"Braxton, what did you think of Parker's performance?" Heidi asked him.

"I'm just glad she's having fun." Braxton said, wording it carefully.

Braxton's P.O.V

Parker and Heidi were trashed. They were both so wasted, but from the huge amount of alcohol they had consumed, I wasn't surprised. In fact, I was impressed by their tolerance.

It was pretty funny, watching them both play drinking games, giggling and having fun, acting their age and forgetting their responsibilities. Well, until they started doing body-shots. Seeing Parker so confident hadn't surprised me at all, I had seen the girl drunk more times than I could count, but I'd never seen her do something so risky before, climbing on top of that other girl was sexy as all hell. I mean, come on, if any man said they didn't enjoy the show, they were flat out lying. Except maybe Chase.

The way Parker made eye contact with me, right before she started, like she wanted to make sure I was watching, it made all the blood drain from my head and shoot to my dick. I hated that there were other men gawking at her, but somehow, it felt like it was just us as well.

I was glad when Chase had suggested going back to the VIP section, to get the girls away from all the men, so far Chase and I had avoided breaking into a fight, with just some glares and strong words, but soon, the men would get drunker, more daring.

Chase was at the bar, whispering in Heidi's ear as she giggled, running her hands over his chest and Parker was in the bathroom as I leaned against the wall, watching Chase with a knowing smirk.

"Get a room!" Parker yelled as she came back in the room.

Heidi turned her head and laughed.

"Done." Chase smiled and picked her up by the thighs so she could wrap her legs around him. She kissed his neck and he carried her off while Parker shuddered.

"So gross." She mumbled and made her way over to me. "Hey Mr Broody." She reached up and bopped me on the nose.

"I'm not broody." I smirked at her.

"You're all lurky, by yourself in the corner." She mimicked my stance, crossing her arms across her chest and putting on her best mean face.

I chuckled at how adorable she looked and turned towards her, relaxing my pose and leaning one arm on the wall, the other at my side. "Where would you rather I be, Princess?"

She shrugged and smiled at me.

"Having a good time?"

"Always." She winked at me and I resisted the urge to pick her up and carry her to another room like Chase did with Heidi.

"Raspberry vodka and a beer?" A busty waitress walked over with a big smile.

"Ohh!" Parker grabbed her red drink and I grabbed the beer, nodding a thank you.

"Anything else I can get you?" She tilted her head and gave me a seductive smile.

"No thanks, love." I chuckled, tipping up the drink.

"Are you-"

"He said he's not interested." Parker snapped, making the waitress jump.

"Sorry Miss Greyson. Sorry Braxton." She mumbled and quickly walked away after Parker sent her another glare.

"Jealous Princess?" I grinned, watching her.

"Puh-lease." She rolled her eyes.

"Mmhmm. Stop denying it babe." I leaned down and placed my lips at her ear. "You want me." I whispered, taking her earlobe between my teeth. Her breath caught in her throat and she lifted her hands to chest on my chest, pushing my cut aside so only the thin fabric of my shirt kept our skin from touching.

"Brax I-" She started, then moaned as I kissed down her neck slowly, placing our drinks on a table. I needed her. I couldn't hold back anymore. The alcohol in my system didn't help either, making me want her that much more.

"You're mine Parker. You always have been. You always will be." I breathed against her soft skin. Fuck, she smelt like fucking heaven.

"Braxton." She moaned, craning her head to the side more.

"Out." I looked up at the two waitresses in the room. They immediately walked out and left us alone. I placed my hands on Parker's hips and moved until our noses were touching. My blue eyes caught her green ones and I lost all control, smashing my lips down on hers. She moaned into my mouth and ran her hands up my chest, looping them around my neck. I pulled her body flush against mine and let my hands travel her gorgeous toned body, finally resting on her perky ass. Tapping my hand lightly, she made a little squealing sound and fell into me more as I chuckled against her lips. My tongue traced her lips and as soon as her mouth opened, I groaned as my dick throbbed in my pants.

She tasted incredible, I would never get used to how good her lips tasted, to how amazing she smelt, to how perfect her small body fit with my big one.

I lifted her by her ass easily and she wrapped around me as I sat on the lounge, leaning back slightly. She moaned as my dick made itself known and she started grinding on top of me, slowly.

"Fuck, Parker." I groaned, breaking the kiss. I tipped my head back and clenched my jaw. Her lips connected with my neck and she started to suck, making me rock her body against me harder.

"Oh God, Brax." She breathed, sitting upright as she moved her hips on me.

Her sexy voice and the sight before me almost made me cream my pants. I slowly moved my fingers to the zipper on her shorts and I stopped, questioning. Her hips stopped moving and she looked into my eyes, like she could see into my soul, if I had one. Her lip went between her teeth and she sighed heavily, looking down and slowly shaking her head.

"I can't Brax." She whispered.

I moved my hands back to her hips lightly and tried to hide the disappointment I felt.

"I just.. I can't. Not here. Not with you. I can't." She mumbled, moving my hands off her completely as she stood up.

"Not with me?" I repeated with a frown, leaning forward to try hide the raging hard on in my pants.

"Parker, lets get more shots!" Heidi laughed, coming back out of the room.

"Sure!" Parker grinned, ignoring me completely. I guess she was done with the conversation. They went to the bar and started pouring themselves shots as Chase sat beside me.

"You good man?" He asked, sensing my annoyed mood.

"Your sister is a piece of work." I blew out a breath and leaned back, having the situation in my jeans under control.

"You already knew that." He chuckled.

"Yeah but.." I trailed off and shook my head.

"She'll come around bro. I know her. She's just scared. It killed her when you went inside."

"I'm not going back." I said firmly.

"You're the right hand man in an MC, man. Since you've been out, you've killed and tortured more people. It's the life we live, Parker included. But, as tough as she seems, it would ruin her if you went back." Chase sighed.

"What's the deal with you and Heidi?" I asked, getting the subject off me and Parker.

"Heidi.. She's a good fuck." He looked over at her and tilted his lips up in a smile when he saw her, laughing hysterically with Parker.

"And?" I pressed.

"And what?" He said, still not looking at me.

"When did you start liking her more than a fuck?" I asked casually.

"What? Bro.. No." Chase's head snapped towards me, fear in his eyes.

"No? Okay, so whens the last time you slept with someone else?" I asked, a smile tugging on my lips.

The fact he had to think about it made me laugh and shake my head.

"It's just sex." He mumbled, in denial.

"Sure man, whatever you say." I chuckled and we both looked at the girls, who had ditched the shot glasses and were drinking straight from the bottle, dancing together and laughing.

"So when are you two going to bone?" Heidi slurred, referring to Parker and I. Clearly they didn't think we could hear, or they were to drunk to remember we were in the room.

"What makes you think we're going to bone?" Parker giggled.

"Oh please! You two have so much sexual tension between you, I could cut it with a knife!" Heidi scoffed.

"That's not true! Brax and I are friends!" Parker took a big gulp of the bottle in her hand.

My mind went back to just before on the couch and earlier today. Didn't seem like just friends to me.

I frowned slightly.

"Why don't you guys just go into the next room and bang each others brains out and get it out of both of your systems?" Heidi continued.

"I'm not going to sleep with him! He's a total man whore anyway." She shrugged.

My jaw locked up and Chase groaned, rubbing his head.

"So what? That generally means they have skills." Heidi laughed, bumping Parker's shoulder.

"Yeah, along with STD's. I told you, I'm getting over my Braxton phase. I will not go back to him. No way." She shook her head vigorously.

"But everyone can tell he really cares about you." Heidi cocked her head to the side.

"I'm just his bosses little sister. It's his job to care about me. Other than that, he doesn't. I'm nothing but a challenge. He's slept with more women than I've even met." She rolled her eyes.

The pain in my chest was worse than all the times I have been shanked or shot. It was like Parker had just reached into my chest and ripped my heart out and thrown it on the fucking ground. My fists clenched and rage filled me. Is that what she really thought?

"He thinks he's so irresistible, but he really just manipulates people. He manipulated me for eleven years and I'm done." Parker held her hands up in surrender.

"Brax." Chase breathed out in shock.

"Don't." I spat out.

He sighed and sent a glare towards his sister.

"What's wrong?" Parker stood in front of me, having the audacity to look concerned in her drunken state.

"You know what Parker? I'm done too. I'm not chasing you anymore. You'll never trust me." I got up so fast she stumbled back a step.

"What?" Her voice shook and she looked up at me with big, confused eyes.

"Go fuck yourself." I spat and walked off, the club parted like the red sea, clearing my path after one look at the rage on my face. As soon as I stepped outside, the cold air whipped my face and I took a deep breath. I was so full of rage that I was shaking, I shoved my hands into my jeans pockets and walked down the street with a brisk pace until some guy ran into me.

"Watch where you're fucking going, dickhead!" He yelled, pushing me back. I froze and turned on him, slowly.

"Big. Fucking. Mistake." I growled.

"Fuck.. Brax.. I'm sorry." He paled, taking a step back.

I swung my fist into his face and punched him, over and over. I shoved him into a wall and punched him in the stomach so hard I heard the crack of his ribs as he screamed in pain.

"Brax!" I heard Chase's voice coming towards me but I had blacked out, punching the man over and over. I pushed him to the ground and got down, hitting him repeatedly.

"Bro, he's had enough." Chase gripped my arms and struggled to yank me up to my feet. I stumbled back into Chase and sighed, closing my eyes, trying to calm down.

"Damn girls, how much?" Another male voice came from behind me and I turned to see Parker and Heidi, leaning on the wall, still wasted. Two men were beside them, trying to grab them.

"Get the fuck away from them!" I snapped at them both, even though I wanted to throttle Parker, I still cared about her and it was my job to protect her.

Chase was able to grab Heidi's arm and he yanked her to his body, but Parker was closer and he couldn't reach her without the other men reaching her first.

"Or what?" One of the men turned to me. "What the fuck happened there?" He pointed at the man I had beaten.

"Get. The fuck. Away. From. Her." I stalked closer.

"Come on gorgeous, let's go." The man ignored me.

I growled and grabbed the one closer to me, throwing him to the floor and clutching the other mans wrist, the hand he was trying to grab Parker with. I bent it and it snapped instantly, then felt a fist connect with my face from the first guy. I spat out blood and swung at them both, hitting them over and over until they were both on the ground, covered in blood and purple welts that were starting to form. My knuckles throbbed but I ignored it.

"You okay?" I asked through clenched teeth, spinning my head at Parker.

She nodded vigorously.

I nodded curtly and turned, walking away, leaving her, Heidi and Chase to clean up my mess. I walked fast and zoned out everything else around me.

****

What do you guys think of the different P.O.V'S?

Whose do you prefer reading in?

DID ANYONE SEE MY CHEEKY LITTLE HIDDEN SECRET THAT I ADDED IN?!

To those of you who saw it; Are you still picking up pieces of your blown mind? ;) Haha :P

What about Parker saying those things? :o (personally, I'm mad at her! My characters have a voice of there own and I just run with it, so I'm very mad at her!) ;) Haha.

Thank you so much for reading my little snicker-doodles!

- Jade xx

Eight Years Later © Khaotik_Angel, 2016

# Chapter Four:

--------------------------------------------------------

I'm not as think as you drunk I am.

- Don't threaten me with a good time - Panic! At The Disco.

Chapter Four:

Parker's P.O.V

I woke up and groaned, pulling my blanket over my head.

What the fuck happened last night?

I was still dressed in my outfit, including the shoes. I don't remember a thing past doing a line of shots with Heidi.

I felt my stomach flip and I quickly waddled to the toilet, emptying my stomach contents into the bowl. I hugged the toilet and groaned again, feeling like absolute death.

I stay like that for awhile, going in and out of consciousness, until I was sure that my stomach was unable to bring anything else up. I finally stood and ran myself a shower, brushing my teeth three times for good measure. I scrubbed my body and hair, then stepped out and dried off, going to gather some clothes. I threw on my purple and black sports bra and some underwear, then pulled on a pair of black yoga pants. I tried to pull my hair into a bun, but I winced as my throbbing headache seemed to spread to each individual hair. I whimpered and left it loose as I slowly walked downstairs, clutching the rail for dear life.

"Good morning sunshine!" Chase yelled as I stepped in the kitchen.

"Shut the fuck up before I shove my knife down your throat." I muttered, gripping the counter top.

"Chase, hurry up." Heidi groaned from beside me, she wore track pants and a tank top, with dark sunglasses on.

"Here." Chase set down a glass for both of us.

"Thank you, Greyson family of alcoholics." I praised, downing the disgusting green hangover cure miracle drink.

"What the fuck happened last night?" I looked at Heidi, then Chase.

"You don't remember?" Chase's eyes widened slightly.

"Last thing I remember was doing a line of shots with her." I pointed to Heidi.

"You don't remember the tequila?" Heidi asked.

"Tequila?" I frowned.

"We did body shots. You made quite a show." She laughed, then whimpered, holding her head.

Flashbacks surfaced of me straddling a girl and making a show of the routine.

"Oh my God." I groaned, placing my head on the counter.

"Did we give you and Brax a hard time?" Heidi asked Chase, then looked at the table.

I followed her gaze to see Braxton sitting there, his long legs kicked up on the table, staring at the ceiling with his jaw clenched and his arms crossed over his chest. He looked pissed off and one of his eye had a dark bruise.

"What happened to you?" I asked Braxton, before Chase could answer.

He didn't answer, he just slowly lowered his gaze and glared at me.

I gulped. His eyes were blazing, his face filled with anger as he looked at me. He's never ever looked at me like that. Other people, sure, but never me.

"Clearly something happened." Heidi said quietly.

"Just Parker being a total bitch, as usual." Chase said.

I looked at him with an eyebrow raised.

"What the fuck did I do?" I glared at him.

Heidi gasped and slapped her hand over her mouth.

I looked at her.

"Brax, I'm so sorry." She looked at him.

He didn't answer.

"What the fuck guys?' I punched the counter top, making everyone jump in surprise.

"Let's go." Heidi grabbed Chase's arm and led him out of the room.

"Fill me in?' I looked at Braxton.

"Forget it." He spat and pushed the table back with his foot as he stood up. The vein in his neck was pulsing and all his muscles were rigid.

"Brax." I reached out and touched his bicep before he could leave.

"Quit it, Parker! I'm nothing but a man whore, remember? All I care about is myself and sex?" He yelled, rounding on me. Making me stumble back a step in shock.

"You really think I only see you as a challenge? That I don't care? That is such bullshit!" He slammed his fist down into the bench beside me and I jumped in surprise.

I stared into his burning blue eyes and then recognition washed over me like an ice cold bucket of water.

The conversation with Heidi, he had heard every word. He had stormed out and when we followed, we found him beating the shit out of a man, covered in blood. He then beat two other guys that were hitting on Heidi and I. He was so angry, so full of rage, then he stormed off.

"Oh my God, Braxton." I gasped and looked up at him.

"Save it. You say I manipulated you, but I never did Parker. You've been the one playing me. You never had any intention to give me a chance, to give us a chance, but you still led me on. Don't pretend to be so fucking innocent." He yelled.

"Brax-" Tears filled and overflowed my eyes, rushing down my face as I reached for him.

"Don't!" He swatted my hand away and sighed, looking deep into my eyes, "From now on, I'm dealing with Chase. Our relationship is strictly business."

"I'm so sorry. I didn't mean it." I sniffed, wanting him to stop looking at me like that, with such hurt and anger. I wanted him to laugh and pull me into his arms. I wanted him to kiss me and hold me. I wanted him.

"Yes. You did." He sighed and ran a hand through his hair, then turned and walked away, leaving me alone.

A strangled sob broke out of my throat and my vision blurred with more tears. I ran blindly upstairs to my room and slammed my door shut, falling on my bed in a pathetic mess of sobs. I gripped my pillow and screamed into it, soaking it with my tears. My heart felt like it had been torn in half inside my chest, the same pain that had filled me the day Braxton had been sentenced.

I heard Heidi's soft knocks on my door a few times over the hours, but I ignored her.

I ignored everyone.

****

Thoughts on this chapter? I know, it was super short and I'm so sorry! But last update was mega long, so that kinda makes up for it, right? (Please don't hurt me)

What do you think of Parker and Braxton's little talk?

Thank you so much for reading my little cheesy puffs!

- Jade xx

Eight Years Later © Khaotik_Angel, 2016

# Chapter Five:

----------------------------------------

I can't suppress it anymore, here it comes like a flood.

- Scream - Thousand Foot Krutch

Chapter Five:

Parker's P.O.V

I hadn't seen Braxton all week. I had hardly left my room, only for food, and even then, I was barely eating. I was ignoring Heidi and Chase and had only spoken to Doug, Sin and Saint a few times, plus some of the other guys in the gang.

I looked in the mirror and tried to fix myself once again. Tonight I had to see Braxton. We had to go to Hector's and get the rest of the money from him. I wore dark jeans, a black tank top and my leather jacket with some black ankle boots with a sharp heel. My makeup was simple and made me look slightly less depressed and my hair was loose.

"Parker, get your fucking ass down here!" Chase bellowed, making me jump. I took a deep breath and slowly left my room.

"Good luck gorgeous." Saint brushed my hair back behind my ear and kissed the top of my head.

I smiled a sad smile at him and he pulled me into a bear hug. I hugged him back, then pulled away and walked downstairs, his loud boots told me he was behind me.

"Bout fucking time." Chase muttered, pulling his gun into his jacket. Fuck. My gun. My knives. My eyes widened. Chase would probably kill me if I told him I left all my stuff in my room, he had no patience with me. As if reading my mind, Saint handed me my stuff. I looked up at him and he smiled a half smile.

"Loaded and ready to go, boss." He winked at me.

"Thank you." I mumbled, grabbing them and concealing them.

"Hurry the fuck up." Chase growled at me. Heidi was beside him and Braxton was leaning against the wall with a cigarette in his mouth, seemingly ignoring me.

"How about you do this you-fucking-self Chase! Don't bark orders at me." I spat at him.

"Don't fucking-" He started yelling, stepping closer to me.

"Guys! Stop!" Heidi got between us, holding her hands up to both of us.

"Do your fucking job, Parker. You may be a Greyson, but I'm still older than you. I'm Alex Greyson's son. You're just the bait." Chase glared at me.

"Don't try intimidate me, Chase. It won't work." I narrowed my eyes at him.

He moved around Heidi and pushed me, making me yip and fall flat on my ass.

"Learn your fucking place." He stared down at me then walked outside.

"You okay?" Heidi asked, trying to pull me up.

"Don't." I yanked my arm away from her and stood up by myself.

"He's just-"

"Shut the fuck up, Heidi. Chase is obviously on Braxton's side, doesn't that mean you should be on mine?" I looked at her, the hurt in my voice was clear.

"Parker-" She stepped forward.

"Heidi, hurry the fuck up!" Chase yelled, starting his car.

She bit her lip, shot me an apologetic look, then ran outside.

"Of course not." I mumbled.

"Hey.. Be careful okay?" Saint grabbed my arm as I went to walk off.

"Whatever." I snatched my arm away and stormed outside, getting in my Range Rover. Braxton walked out calmly and got in his car, revving the engine. I ground my teeth together and wished, not for the first time, that I could shoot lasers out of my eyes.

I grumbled and got out of my car, slamming the door a little to hard and I stomped over to his car, crossing my arms over my chest.

We drove in silence the whole time. He fiddled with the stereo and then Led Zeppelin's Stairway To Heaven came on. Braxton loved this song. I loved it as well, we used to always listen to it together. It was the extended version, obviously, you can't just listen to the cut version without the solos, it was blasphemy. I looked out the window, not wanting to look at him, not wanting him to see how hurt I really was.

He stopped the car and climbed out instantly, leaving me in the car. I huffed out a breath and got out as well, running to keep up with his long strides. He knocked on the garage door and one of Hector's guys stood there, looking between us.

"Hector!" He called, ushering us inside.

"P-Parker. Braxton. Good to see you two." Hector came into the garage.

"How's the finger, Hector?" I cocked my head to the side, putting on my business face.

"It's going well, Parker. I apologize for my behavior. I should of shown you more respect and not tried to.." He trailed off.

"Fuck me?" I finished for him.

He nodded, turning red.

"Give me my money, Hector." I sighed and leaned against the wall lazily.

"Here." He reached into his drawer and fished out an envelope, handing it to me with a shaky hand. Braxton took it and sifted through it.

"It better be there, Hector. For your sake. I'm not in the mood." I glared at him.

"Six." Braxton told me in his deep voice that gave me shivers.

"Good job, Hector!" I grinned at him.

"O-Of course." He nodded.

"Well, it's been a pleasure. If you want to do business with the Knights again, talk to me and Chase." I winked.

"T-Thank you Parker." He looked down, terrified.

I ran my hand through his hair then left, knowing Braxton was following behind me. I walked over to the car and climbed in beside him. He tossed the envelope of money into my lap and I sifted through it.

"I checked it." He looked at me for the first time.

"I know, I'm just double checking." I mumbled.

"Right, I forgot how untrustworthy I am." He scoffed.

"Braxton-"

His phone buzzed, interrupting me.

"Hello?" He held his phone to his ear.

"Oh, hey gorgeous." He smirked.

My heart sank.

"Yeah I can come by, I just finished work."

"I'm on my way." He said then hung up, pulling away from the curb.

"Where are we going?" I asked when he passed the road to get back home.

"I'm going to see someone." He said without looking at me.

"Can you drop me off at home first?" I looked at him.

"I could but I'm not planning on spending the night with her. You can wait in the car." He said evenly.

"Seriously? You want me to wait in the car while you go fuck some random girl?" I spat out.

"Just living up to my reputation, Parker. Don't be so surprised." He said, his words were like ice.

He was getting back at me.

I ground my teeth and he pulled up on the curb, getting out, he walked casually over to the door. A blonde opened the door and dove on him, wrapping her legs around him and kissing him instantly. He held her body to his and kissed her back, walking inside and kicking the door closed.

Tears leaked out of my eyes and I put my fist into my mouth to try stop the loud sobs from leaving me. I waited there for half an hour, then wiped my tears away, swallowing deeply.

"Why the fuck should I wait for him?" I said to myself. I reached over and sighed in relief. The keys were stuffed in the seat. I scooted over and turned the key, making the car roar to life. I pressed my foot on the gas and peeled away from the curb, away from him.

I sped home and ran inside, going straight upstairs and into my room. I threw the keys on my cupboard with the envelope. I stripped off and pulled on a sports bra and some little black yoga shorts then got into bed and cried into my pillow.

"Parker!" The blanket was ripped off of my body and I fumbled to sit up, rubbing my eyes open.

"Brax?" I looked up at him, in confusion. He looked furious. The events of last night flickered in my mind and I instantly felt hurt all over again.

"You stole my fucking car. You left me stranded!" He growled.

I stood up and walked to the bathroom, brushing my teeth and washing my face.

"I didn't steal it. You left the keys inside." I shrugged.

"Parker!" He sent his fist into the door frame, making the wall shake.

"What did you expect me to do?!" I whirled around to face him.

He looked a little shocked at my outburst.

"Did you seriously just expect me to sit there and wait for you? You didn't just cross the line last night, Braxton. You broke it in fucking half." I stared at him. "I understand I hurt you and I'm sorry. But last night you really hurt me." I walked past him and grabbed his keys, tossing them to him. He caught them automatically and then gulped, looking a little ashamed. Good.

"Parker.. I'm sorry. I went way to far." He said quietly, like he only just realized.

"I forgive you." His face brightened, looking hopeful and surprised.

I looked down at the floor and continued, "But you ruined any chance of anything happening between us."

"What?" His voice was hoarse and full of disbelief.

"You're my brothers best friend. You're the second in command to the Knights. We work side by side and you're my friend. That's it. That's all you will ever be. I can't. Not after last night." I breathed, feeling tears fill my eyes.

"But I need you." He sounded so lost and broken.

I swallowed back the lump in my throat and didn't answer.

"When I was inside, the thing that got me through was knowing you cared about me. I wanted to make you mine officially when I got out. Parker, we belong together." He touched my arm and I flinched, making him drop his arm to his side.

"Parker.. Please. I'll do anything. You know we belong together." He pleaded.

I shook my head.

"Look at me." He gently pulled my chin up to look into his gorgeous face. I wanted to hug him and never let him go, but I knew I couldn't.

"I can't." I breathed.

"You can't tell me you don't feel this." He stroked my cheek, sending sparks through me. "You feel it. I know you do." He begged.

"It doesn't matter." I gently tugged his hand down from my face.

"Yes, it does. You matter, we matter. I'd do anything for you, for us. Princess, please." His eyes were huge, hopeful and sad.

"Please, just go." I tried to push back.

"No." He growled and then his lips were on mine, kissing me deeply. I tried to push him away but my body took over, reacting to him immediately, winding my arms around him and twisting my tongue with his. After a few Earth shattering minutes, I pushed back.

"Please, leave." I cried.

"Princess-"

"Go." I sobbed and ran back into my bathroom, slamming the door shut and sinking against it, hugging my knees and crying my heart out.

****

*Braces self for hate comments*

I APOLOGIZE ON BRAXTON'S BEHALF GUYSSSS!

I would like to dedicate this chapter to another one of my best friends  , my little Minxy Moo!  She is an incredibly talented and beautiful person! If you are into romance/drama/mystery stuff with a hell of a lot of sexual tension and steam, SHE IS YOUR GIRL! Head on over and check her out! Tell her I sent you ;)

What do you think of this situation?

What about Parker's reaction?

Thank you so much for reading my little cherries! (I guess this is a thing now haha)

- Jade xx

Eight Years Later © Khaotik_Angel, 2016

# Chapter Six:

-------------------------------------------------------------

Isn't it messed up, how I'm just dying to be him?

- Sugar, we're going down - Fall Out Boy

Chapter Six:

Braxton's P.O.V

I held my glass in my hand, nursing it gently as I lounged in the VIP room. It had been a few days since Parker had basically ripped my heart out of my chest and spat on it, making sure to stomp on it with those sexy sharp high heels she wears. I hadn't seen her since. Granted, most of my time had been spent in this very bar, drinking away my sorrows so the days passed in a drunken blur.

I had fucked up. I had fucked up bad.

My phone buzzed in my pocket and I pulled it out, pressing it to my ear.

"Brax?" A girly voice asked when I didn't say anything.

"Who is this?" I frowned.

"Jasmine." She giggled.

My frown deepened. Jasmine?

"You came over the other night?" She supplied when I didn't respond.

"Oh. Hi." I sighed and rubbed my temples.

"Do you wanna come over baby?" She purred.

"I'm busy."

"You seem tense.. I'm sure I could help with that." She said in a seductive voice.

"No." I growled and hung up, pushing my phone back into my pocket. That bitch was why Parker hated me. Okay, so maybe it was all my fault and I shouldn't blame this Jasmine girl for my fuck up, but I didn't care.

"You okay, sugar?" The blonde behind the bar asked, pouring me another drink.

I grunted and tipped it back, sliding it back to her for a refill. She obliged, looking at me with worry.

I sighed and eventually finished that drink as well, standing and walking to my Harley, riding back to the mansion, not even caring that I was in no state to drive. I got off the bike and heard loud music from the backyard.

Curiosity got the better of me and I walked back there. Some girls were in the pool or tanning on the side in skimpy bikinis, or less and a few of the guys were in the water. More of the guys were spread out, making out with girls, smoking and drinking. Most of the gang was here. I noticed Chase's back up on the grass, away from everyone and I walked over.

"Hey man." I muttered.

"Are you drunk?" He looked over to me.

"Had a couple." I shrugged.

"My sister isn't very happy. I'm assuming you have something to do with that?" He asked, looking straight ahead.

"Spot on." I grumbled and kicked up a tuff of grass.

"Fuck you, Parker!" A man, Victor, yelled suddenly.

I frowned in confusion at the sound and my eyes set on Parker, running ahead of him with Heidi trailing quite far behind.

She skidded to a stop in front of Chase and I and gracefully hopped to the side when Victor tried to tackle her down.

"Such a sore loser." She shook her head.

"My legs are longer than yours, how are you so fast?" He panted from the ground.

"She's been training since she was about five. That's why." Chase laughed.

"Next!" Parker looked at Chase, ignoring me completely. She was wearing a black and blue sports bra and black gym shorts with pink and black Nike's on, her hair pulled into a ponytail. God, she was so beautiful.

"Victor, get up. I want you to fight her." Chase said suddenly.

"What? Boss, no. I don't want to hurt her!" Victor jumped to his feet.

"Bitch, please." Parker rolled her eyes.

"Victor, just do it." Chase tuned in.

"Damn guys," Heidi panted, just now getting to us.

"Come at me, Viccy." Parker taunted.

"Parker.." He trailed off, looking pained.

She sighed and, quick as lightening, sent her foot into his side, knocking him to the side.

"Ow!" He clutched his side.

"I barely touched you, get up." She frowned.

"Fine." He spat and lunged at her. She dodged him easily and giggled.

Parker had always been a great fighter, but her skill had improved so much since she was seventeen. Chase trained her well.

Victor grunted and launched at her again, she skipped away again and looked at him, a glint in her beautiful green eyes.

"Stay still." He growled.

"Catch me if you can." She winked, playing with him.

He slowly walked over to her, trying to intimidate her by getting all up in her face. She didn't move as he stalked around her, her smile never faltered.

He sent his arm out to connect with her chest, but she ducked quickly and sent a swift kick in his back, making him stumble.

"Come on Victor, stop going easy in me!" She tipped her head back, teasing his skill.

He was a very sluggish fighter, he sat towards the bottom of the ranks. He sent his fist into her face but she caught it and yanked him to her. She twisted his arm and he yelled out in pain. Parker pushed him back before she broke it and sighed, getting bored.

"Hey Boss." A man came to stand at Chase's other side.

"Damen." He nodded.

"How is she?" He asked.

"She's bored." Chase laughed.

"Hey Parker." This Damen guy called.

"Hey Damen!" She grinned at him.

"Kicking his ass?"

Her grin widened.

"What have I told you about playing with your opponents? Just end them." He laughed.

"That's no fun!" She giggled.

"Damen, jump in. See how she goes." Chase mumbled.

"Yes sir." Damen walked over and smiled at Parker.

"Let's go." She sent a kick into Victor's stomach and Damen launched at her, clearly a much better fighter than Victor.

"Whose that?" I asked.

"Damen. He trains Parker and shows her how to do a lot of the new fighting techniques." Chase explained.

I watched as Parker dodged it and sent her foot into his back. He grabbed her leg and yanked it from under her, making her land on the grass. She jumped up and sent her fist into his face quickly, sending him stumbling back a step. Victor grabbed her arms from behind her, pinning her against him. Damen jabbed her stomach and the air left her. She struggled but couldn't fight Victor's larger frame.

She sent her foot down into his and he let her go, yelping. Parker sent her elbow back into his face and then kicked up on Damen's chest, booting him away from her, she skipped away from both men, her chest heaving.

"Good job Parker." Damen smiled, standing back up.

Victor went for Parker and she hopped to the side, grabbing his arm and yanking, using his own strength against him. She bent his arm and sent him to his knees, pulling him into a headlock.

"Fuck." He choked out in defeat, tapping out. She let him go and got to her feet, facing Damen.

He sent his foot into her stomach and she flew back, landing in a heap on top of Victor who wheezed in pain as he caught her.

"Thanks Vic." She gasped out, wincing as she stood up. He grumbled something and coughed, clutching his body.

"Stop showing you're hurt." Chase encouraged her.

She straightened her back and glared at Damen.

"You can't show weakness. They will use it against you." Damen tuned in.

Parker sent her fist out and Damen caught it so she flung her other fist into his head, making him groan and stumble, holding his head. She quickly kicked him to the ground and pushed her foot into his throat. He grabbed her foot and ripped it out from under her, making her fall and straddle him.

He flipped the position so he was hovering over her and she yipped in shock.

"Not a good idea. Especially when you're fighting men." He told her.

She lifted her knee in his crutch and he fell back as Chase and I winced. She jumped up and sent her fist into his face, so he fell flat on his back and she booted him so he flipped onto his stomach. She sat on him and pulled his wrists into one of her hands, grabbing his neck and pulling him into a twisted headlock. It would only take one jerk and she could snap his neck.

"Okay, I give." He managed to choke out.

She let him go and rolled off him, panting as she stared at the sky.

"Woo! Go Parker!" Heidi cheered.

"That was good." Damen sat up, leaning on his knees.

"She's still not strong enough." Chase said between clenched teeth.

"Chase.. You need to understand, she can't become as strong as you or Braxton, or the twins. She isn't as strong." Damen said carefully.

"So what happens if someone built like us tries to grab her?" He stepped forward and Damen visibly gulped.

"I'll shoot." Parker said, getting to her feet.

"I want you stronger." He shook his head.

"Chase." She groaned and he suddenly lunged at her, picking her up and throwing her into the ground harshly, the thud echoing. The air left her and she curled into a ball from the pain, her eyes squeezing shut.

"Exactly." Chase sighed and bent down, picking her up carefully. She winced and I saw tears in her eyes from the pain.

"Chase, she can't get as big as you." Heidi tried.

"I want her to be able to protect herself." He glared at her.

Parker sent her elbow into Chase's stomach and she hopped out of his grip, sending her foot into his stomach to boot him. He caught her foot and spun it so she was twisted. He dropped her and she landed with another thud.

Parker was a good fighter, that much was clear, she was fast and good at using her opponents strength against them, but Chase was right, if she ever had to deal with a guy like me or Chase, she was done for. That made me very nervous.

She got to her feet slowly and looked at Chase, she was clearly in a lot of pain from all her falls, plus her fight with Victor and Damen.

"I'm sorry gorgeous." Chase softened and hugged her gently, rubbing her back.

"I'm good with a gun." She grumbled stubbornly, pulling back.

"You are." He smiled at her. Say what you want about Chase Greyson, about his methods and his anger issues, but Parker was his whole world. He loved her more than anything. She was all the blood related family he had left, she reminded him of their mum and he would do anything for her.

"Understatement of the fucking century. What aren't you good at Parker?" Heidi rolled her eyes.

"Everything that isn't to do with my training." She mumbled, a little sadly, looking down.

I clenched my jaw. That was a lie. Parker had so many talents. She was so smart and sexy, but also so cute and beautiful, all at the same time. I liked that she was so sassy and edgy, her smart ass attitude and the fight she had in her was one of the main draws I had to her. She was fearless, she could have a guy five times her size standing there and she'd still yell her mind at him and smack him if she felt he deserved it.

We were both so damaged, so caught up in this life that we knew we could never leave. How couldn't she see how perfectly we matched each other?

"I'm hungry." Heidi complained.

"Me too." Chase sighed.

"I'm in." Parker rubbed her stomach.

"Brax?" Chase looked at me.

"Sure." I shrugged a shoulder.

Chase lifted Parker suddenly, flipping her gently over his shoulder and carrying her towards the house. She squealed and laughed, trying to struggle. I laughed and Heidi and I followed them.

"Oh shit." Chase muttered.

I looked around him and felt my body tense.

"What?" Parker asked, sensing our reservation. Chase turned suddenly so she was facing Jesse. He stared at her, confused, hurt and a little pissed.

"Jesse?" She breathed.

"Did you drop off the fucking planet? I've been trying to call you for two fucking weeks!" He glared at her.

"I was busy." She said blankly.

She hadn't spoken to him.. The whole time we were fighting. The thought made me smile slightly.

"For two weeks?" He raised his eyebrows.

She sighed and pushed against Chase, who put her down. She straightened her outfit and glared at him.

"Yes. For two weeks." She placed her hand on her hip. None of us budged, we wanted to hear this. All of us.

"What have you been doing?" He pressed.

"It's none of your fucking business." She scoffed.

"I can't work you out." He shook his head. "You're the only girl I've met with such raging commitment issues."

"Commitment issues? She spluttered. "What fucking commitment?!"

"You know I like you, Parker! It's not like I haven't tried with you, but you just act dumb."

"Take that as a hint maybe?" She laughed once.

"You care about me." He shook his head vigorously.

"There is a huge difference between sex and a relationship!" She yelled.

"It's more than sex."

"Not for me. That's all it ever was." Her voice was stone cold.

"What are you so scared of? Who hurt you so badly that you can't let anyone in?" He frowned and took a step towards her.

I gulped. That would be me.

"I'm not scared of anything." She said between clenched teeth.

"You pretend to be this hard shelled bad girl but I'm trying to get to know you."

"You'll never get to know me. It was just sex, Jesse, but in complete honesty, sex with you isn't even worth the drama." She crossed her arms over her chest.

I grinned, I couldn't help it, I just let it fill my face.

"You're lying." He narrowed his eyes at her.

"Whatever helps you sleep at night. Look, for a normal girl, I'm sure you're fine and they don't find you completely predictable and boring. But I'm different. Sorry stud." She shrugged and turned, walking into the kitchen with a non caring face.

Jesse just gaped.

"You should leave." Chase stifled a laugh.

He looked at Chase, then his eyes landed on me. "This is your fault."

"What?" I scoffed.

"I don't know why or how. But you did this to her, didn't you? As soon as you come back into town, she's totally different." He looked into my eyes, searching for an explanation.

"Get off the property." I said, my voice hard.

"Don't blame Braxton for this." Chase warned.

"Braxton?" Jesse frowned, baffled. Then his eyes widened and he looked at me. "You're Braxton?!" He shouted.

I raised an eyebrow at him, utterly confused.

"Jesse! Get out!" Parker rushed in and yelled, looking panicked.

"This is Braxton?!" He turned to her.

She fumbled for words, her face blushing slightly.

"You told me he was just an ex? You forgot to mention he is your brothers best friend and you see him every day!" Jesse continued.

"Parker? What the fuck?" Chase asked in confusion.

Then it hit me. I spun my head and looked at Parker, aware my jaw was probably on the floor and my eyes were popping out of my skull. "You kept it?" My voice was thick with emotion.

She glanced at me and our eyes connected, making my knees weak.

"The fuck is going on?" Chase demanded.

"This!" Jesse reached over and pulled on the elastic of Parker's gym shorts, pulling one side down a few inches.

There it was. My name with the heart. Sitting there, proud and bold against her flawless skin.

"Ohh." Chase drew it out. "I forgot about that."

"Have you been sleeping with him since he got back?" Jesse yelled at her.

She didn't seem to hear him, her eyes were locked with mine, like we were in a trace.

She kept it.

She could of easily gotten it covered up, or removed, but she didn't. She kept it.

"Well?!" Jesse demanded again.

She didn't say anything.

"Parker?!" He yelled in her face, making her blink and look at him.

"Huh?"

"Are you sleeping with him?! Have you been sleeping with him this whole time?" Jesse repeated.

"What? No." Parker frowned and shook her head.

"I don't believe you. You have his name tattooed in your skin. He means something to you."

"I don't care if you believe me or not. I kept the tattoo because I was in love with him. But, then I kept it as a reminder. To not open up and trust someone. To love someone. Because they either leave you, or hurt you. Or both." She said to him, but stared right into my eyes.

"Doug!" She called out.

"Yes Boss?" He jogged over and took in the situation.

"Escort Jesse off of the property. Make sure he doesn't come back." She mumbled and just like that, Jesse was hauled out of there.

"Come on." Chase breathed, grabbing Heidi and pulling her into another room, leaving me with Parker.

My body moved without me telling it to. I walked over to Parker and pulled down the side of her shorts, seeing the tattoo again. I ran my thumb over the ink and then looked back up at her.

"Get off me.." She warned.

I shook my head slowly. "You kept it. Say what you want about your reasoning.. But you kept it. You care." I said, my voice hoarse.

"Braxton-"

I smashed my lips down on hers and moaned into her mouth, clutching her hips tighter, pulling her body to me. She kissed me back instantly and her hands went to my chest, trying to push me away but I wasn't having any of it. I needed her. I deepened the kiss and wrapped my arms fully around her. She was mine, my name was literally injected into her flesh, just like hers was in mine.

"Brax." She said into my mouth, trying to pull away. Then she suddenly shoved my chest and sent her fist into my face.

I groaned, clutching my jaw and stumbling back a step. "What the fuck, Park?"

"Braxton, I can't.. I told you, we can't happen." She said, her voice unsteady.

"Why? Baby, come on.. It's me. We're meant for each other." I stared into her eyes, trying to make her see.

"Brax please." Her eyes filled with tears, she looked so defeated, so broken.

"Being apart is killing us both." I stated.

"Brax!" Chase came out the room, shoving his guns into his jacket.

"What's up?" I asked on alert.

"You sober now?" He stood in front of me.

"Yeah." I frowned in confusion. I had sobered up as soon as I laid eyes on Parker.

"I need you with me. Just got an anonymous call. We need to get to the bar." He said.

"What about me?" Parker asked.

"I need you here Park, I'll take some of the boys and Brax, but you're in charge here. I can't risk you leaving here and the compound being attacked." Chase turned to her.

She nodded and Heidi rushed down, handing her a grey tank top and her weapons, Parker jumped into action and I nodded to Chase, signaling I was ready.

"I'll be in touch." He turned and hugged Parker, kissed Heidi deeply, then left.

"Be safe." I stared at Parker, not wanting to leave her.

"You too. Watch his back." She looked at me.

"Always." I pulled her in for a kiss and then left her to go with Chase.

****

Bloody hell! That was one eventful chapter!

What did you guys think?!

What about Parker's mad skills? ;) Slay girl, slay.

I want to dedicate this chapter to  who is a great friend of mine. Hannah was my first ever real fan for my first story, and she has supported me ever since, with every project I have had! Girl, you have no idea how grateful I am for you. You gave me so much love and you made me not give up! I don't think I would be where I am now if it weren't for you. Everyone should go check out Hannah's works! She is very talented and she has some amazing projects up! Plus, the girl is just plain hilarious! Love you my little Hannah cake <3

Thank you so much for reading my little cinnamon buns!

- Jade xx

Eight Years Later © Khaotik_Angel, 2016

# Chapter Seven:

----------------------------------------------------------------

Now these towns, well they all know our name.

The death punch sound is our claim to fame.

- Bad Company - Five Finger Death Punch

Chapter Seven:

Parker's P.O.V

Chase and Braxton burst through the door with all their men behind them. My eyes scanned them both and I sighed in relief, seeing them bloody, but unharmed. Somehow, I doubted the blood was theirs.

"Meeting. Now!" Chase bellowed, walking straight over to Heidi and I. Everyone quickly obeyed Chase's order and scrambled out of the room.

"Anything happen here?" He asked me.

"A couple bikes rode passed, checking if we were here, but nothing else." I told him.

"Good. Come on." He grabbed Heidi and kissed her, then kissed the top of my head, all of us walking into the lounge room. Heidi held back as the three of us went to the front of the room to give the orders. The entire club shut up and looked at us expectantly.

"As of right now, we are in lock down. No one is to leave or come here unless one of us three approve it!" Chase yelled out to everyone. "All of you with wives and kids at home, I want them all here. We've been targeted." He continued.

"What happened at the club Boss?" Doug spoke up from within the crowd.

Chase looked down, then looked back out at everyone. "Club was shot up. I managed to grab one of the assholes and he's in the shed. We need to band together now. As a brotherhood. A family. Any and all arguments between members at the moment, are swept to the side. If you had a punch up yesterday, be prepared to take a bullet for that same brother tomorrow. Lay low and be prepared for war at any time."

"What club are we against?" Sin asked.

"Thieves Den." Chase said evenly.

"How do you know?" Saint tuned in.

"Because it was carved into one of the waitress's backs at the bar." Chase said after a slight hesitation.

Thieves fucking Den. They are our clubs biggest rival.

"Get your families safe boys." I called out and they started to leave the room.

Heidi came over to us and hugged Chase tightly.

"Where do you want me?" I asked.

"I want you to be here when the girls get here. You and Heidi are in charge of making sure they are comfortable when they get here. They will react better to you two then the guys. You can calm them down." Chase told me, holding Heidi in his arms.

"Yes Boss." She whispered, sounding scared. Heidi used to date one of the guys in the Thieves Den, he was a sadistic asshole and Chase and I had saved her from him as soon as we found out she was being beaten.

"Hey, nothing is going to happen." He tipped her chin up to look at him.

"I'll die before I let them touch you." I tuned in.

"You trust me, right?" Chase asked.

She nodded.

"Then trust that I will always protect you, okay?"

She smiled and nodded.

"That's my girl." He winked and kissed her.

My eyebrows rose and I shared a glance with Braxton, who looked just as shocked.

Heidi walked off and Chase turned to us.

"Your girl?" I grinned.

"Shut up, Parker." He scowled. "I mean it. You two need to put everything behind you right now. I need you both in control and not at each others throats." He looked between us.

"Of course, Chase. The Knights are our number one priority right now." Brax said.

"Good. Now lets go see what we can get out of this cocksucker." Chase looked at Braxton.

"Torture and a brewing war. It's good to be home." Braxton laughed darkly.

"Don't kill him." I told them. "We can't afford to be impulsive. Keep him alive for awhile until we get what we need."

Chase nodded. "Look after Heidi, Park. She's freaking out. You two are the glue in this place. You hold the boys together and the wives and kids love you both. If they see Heidi in pieces, they will fall apart."

"I'll sort it all out." I smiled looked him and Braxton over once more. "You two are okay right? No wounds?"

"Not our blood." Braxton mumbled, looking down at his clothes.

"Those poor people. Thieves Den will pay for this." I said in a hard voice.

"Got that right." Chase growled, then walked off with Braxton at his side.

I took a deep breath and went into the kitchen, finding Heidi in there, cooking up a feast.

"Need help?" I came up beside her and peaked into the frying pan full of chicken she was cooking.

"You can go have a shower and get changed." Heidi chuckled, looking at me.

I looked down to see I was still in my gym clothes with a tank top on. I laughed and kissed her cheek, running upstairs and having a quick shower. I pulled on a pair of dark jeans, a grey tank top that hung loose around me, and my leather jacket. Making sure my weapons were concealed and at the ready, I walked downstairs to see some of the guys come through with their wives and kids.

"Parker!" Melanie, Doug's sister came running over to me and hugged me.

"Hey Mel." I hugged her back.

"Can you tell me why that knucklehead dragged me out of my house?" She shot a glare towards her older brother.

"We're on lock down." I sighed.

"Is everything okay? Where are the guys?" She looked around, looking for Sin probably. The two have had a very on and off relationship, much to Doug's horror.

Mel was one of the sweetest girls, with her long blonde hair and bright blue eyes. She had nothing really to do with the club, but she was a good friend, like a little sister to everyone. At twenty one, she was studying to be a nurse and spent all her free time in her bedroom, studying. It was ironic that she was such a sweet, innocent girl, and she had an on and off relationship with a guy named Sin.

"The guys are fine. Saint, Sin, Chase and Brax are just handling something right now." I said carefully, not wanting to mention that they were probably torturing our guest for information.

She nodded and walked with me into the kitchen, helping Heidi with the food while I calmed everyone down.

"We're lucky to have you, Park." Doug mumbled, coming to stand beside me against the counter.

I looked up at him with a raised eyebrow.

"You keep the peace. You soothe all the girls and the kids." He nodded to where everyone was laughing and talking, perfectly calm now.

"It's what a good leader and woman does." I shrugged.

There were more voices and a group of girls came inside with two of the guys. Club whores. We had to keep them safe as well, they were joined to the MC.

"Where's Chase?" One of them, Candy, asked me with a flirty smile.

"He's busy." Heidi said in a hard voice, coming to stand at my other side. I stifled a laugh at her tone.

"Actually, he's not." Chase walked in and smirked at Candy. Being President, Chase got a lot of attention from the girls.

"Hey Chase." She said seductively.

"Parker, Heidi." Chase looked at us and nodded his head, signalling he wanted to talk. We followed him, Brax, Saint and Sin to Chase's office and all sat down.

"What did you get?" I asked him.

"Nothing." Chase sighed and rubbed his forehead.

"He ain't talking. Just being a smart ass." Saint tuned in.

"Did he say anything about..?" Heidi trailed off in a small voice.

"He mentioned you and Parker, yes. But I think it was more to piss us off than an actual threat." Chase looked at Heidi.

"What did he say?" I frowned.

"That Thieves Den want you both. That's about all I got right now." He waved his hand in annoyance.

"What about.. Trigger?" Heidi mumbled, her eyes in her lap.

"Nothing about Trigger." Chase looked at her.

"Whose Trigger?" Braxton asked.

Chase hesitated and looked at me to explain.

"Trigger is one of the Thieves Den boys. Heidi dated him when I first met her. When I became close with her, I started noticing things. Didn't take long to work out he was beating her.. Raping her.. I got Heidi to spill it to Chase and I and we took care of it. He left her alone ever since."

"You didn't kill him?" Braxton looked surprised.

"Didn't think it was necessary at the time. He was just a hotshot. I threatened him and beat the shit out of him and that was it." Chase shrugged.

"Do you really think he would come back for her?" I frowned, putting my arm around my best friend.

"I think he would be stupid enough to try." Chase looked at Heidi, worry in his eyes as he saw how upset she was.

"Heidi, you got nothing to worry about. Anyone here would die for you. You're family, girl." Saint kissed the top of her head and put his arm over her shoulders as well.

"Exactly. The Knights are a brotherhood. But you and Park are our sisters. Even if it wasn't my duty, I'd take a bullet for both of you." Sin tuned in.

"We need to get more info on that douche." I mumbled, pointing in the direction the shed was in.

"Brax and I are going to keep at him. Each day will get worse. He will spill." Chase nodded.

"Keep the families here. We stay under lock down. No one leaves the compound without our say so. Make sure the boys are ready at any moment." I announced.

"Parker's right. We should be preparing for the worst. Make use of the gym and the firing range." Braxton nodded, looking at me.

I quickly looked away.

"Melanie's here." I stared at Sin.

He shrugged a shoulder.

"So keep your dick out of everyone else while she's here." I narrowed my eyes.

"She's not mine. It's not her business where I put my dick."

"I wasn't asking." My voice was hard.

"You can't order me to not fuck anyone." Sin laughed.

"Try me." I leaned forward. "That girl is the best fucking thing that came into your miserable life and you know you will never find anyone like her again. Don't hurt her, Sin."

"She's got a point bro." Saint sighed.

"She's not involved in this shit. She's a fucking nurse. I can't corrupt her." Sin muttered.

"You should of thought about that before you first stuck your dick up her then." I snapped.

"Parker-" Chase started.

"You wouldn't understand. You have Braxton. You two are just as deadly as each other. Don't lecture me about just getting with Mel when you can't even accept to be with Brax after eleven years. You two are clearly in love with each other!" Sin yelled, standing up. "If I got with Mel, she'd just worry that I wouldn't come back to her after a run, you don't have to worry about that."

"No, instead I have to worry about either of us getting thrown in fucking prison!" I jumped up too. "You have no fucking idea what I went through when it came to Braxton! Eight years! I was miserable for eight fucking years! I was never allowed to see him, I was never allowed to speak to him. I just had to sit there and wait. You all know for a fact I never moved on and I probably never will. But don't fucking judge me cause you have no idea what I went through."

Everyone was silent at my outburst.

"You don't think it killed me seeing him get sent away? You think it didn't destroy me every time Chase set up for one of the club girls to go fuck him? You all expect me to be so mellow about Brax cause I love him, but sometimes that isn't enough." I mumbled the last part as a tear fell down my cheek.

"Parker-" Sin looked at me, brokenly.

"Appreciate what you have with Mel. Don't let her get away." I looked down.

"Give us a minute." Braxton muttered.

The sound of chairs scrapping, then footsteps as they left the room filled my ears, then it was silent.

"You don't think it killed me as well?" He said after a minute of silence. "You really think that as soon as the judge sentenced me, you weren't going through my head? You were all that was going through my head. I knew I wouldn't be able to talk to you or see you, for eight years and that ripped me apart." He got up and slowly walked over to where I was standing.

"I had nothing to remind me of you so I focused on all the memories we had together. I thought of you everyday. I had no idea if you had moved on from me, if you stopped caring. I made myself believe you still cared, cause that's what pulled me through. When Chase sent me girls, I was miserable. I'm not going to say I didn't enjoy the sex, cause that would be a lie. But they were nothing to me. You were my world. Every time I got a letter or a visitor, I wished it was you even though I knew it wouldn't be." He continued, slowly grabbing my hands in his.

"At least you knew I loved you." I looked up at him.

"You never said the words but yeah. I knew. I should of told you how I felt." He sighed.

"How you felt?" I raised an eyebrow.

He thought for a minute, then pulled his cut off.

"What are you doing?" I frowned as he pulled his shirt off, exposing his muscled, tattooed torso. I swallowed and tried not to drool everywhere.

"I got this just before I got sentenced." He mumbled and slowly pulled my hand up to touch his chest.

Parker. My Princess.

Three words with a matching heart at the end. I traced over the letters with my fingertips and looked up at him, tears leaving my eyes.

"I didn't have time to show you after I was put away." He said sadly. "Baby, I'm so sorry."

"Brax I-"

"I know. You aren't ready yet. But just know that you are mine. Just like I'm yours. Take your time, but don't say we have no chance. Sin is an idiot, but he was right about one thing; we're made for each other. We waited for eight years of our lives and we are still as love struck as we were back then. I'm fine with waiting some more, for you. For us." Braxton said, his deep voice rumbling through to my very core, filling me with warmth.

All I could do was nod.

"That's my girl." He smiled and kissed my forehead gently. I stood up on my tiptoes and wrapped my arms around his neck, kissing him deeply. He made a surprised noise and held my hips, kissing me back automatically. Tears continued to leak out of my eyes, I could taste them in the kiss.

This very man had just come back from torturing a man and yet, his lips were so soft, his hands so gentle and his body so inviting. He pulled back slightly and both of us were out of breath, his forehead resting against my own.

"If I see you with another slut, I will not hesitate to tear your dick from your body." I breathed, my eyes still closed, a ghost of a smile on my face.

"Deal." He laughed a breathy laugh and pulled me into a warm embrace.

"Do you think it will be difficult to get information out of that guy?" I asked, snuggling into his bare chest, feeling all his hard muscles.

"Shouldn't be to hard. I'm the King of torture, remember? I'm pretty twisted and creative." He chuckled darkly.

"True." I laughed and kissed the tattoo over his heart.

****

What do you think of Sin?! And what about him and Mel?

Parker and Braxton's chat?

Who is your favourite character?! I'd love to know!

Thank you so much for reading my little bunny rabbits!

- Jade xx

Next chapter is going to be very.. Intense.. And not in a sexual way haha. It will be a little gory, so don't be all "ahhh, wtf Jade!" Hahaha, fair warning ;)

Eight Years Later © Khaotik_Angel, 2016

# Chapter Eight:

------------------------------------------------

Welcome to a day in my life.

    - A Day In My Life - Five Finger Death Punch

Chapter Eight:

Braxton's P.O.V

"What does the Den want with the Knights?!" I yelled into his face. This cunt was really pissing me off now.

"Heidi and Parker's tight pussy, for one." He laughed, coughing up blood.

I grabbed a metal bat and sent it into his ribs, over and over, making him yell out in pain.

"One more fucking time. What the fuck does the Den want with the Knights?!" Chase yelled from beside me.

"Have you fucked her yet, Braxton? What does she feel like? I bet she feels like fucking heaven." He smirked at me.

I turned and grabbed a syringe, plunging it into him and injecting him full of the drug. Something to slow his heart rate so he wouldn't die on us. I grabbed my pocket knife and sliced down his bicep that was hung up and chained to the ceiling.

"Here, hold this." I mumbled and sent the knife into his leg, making sure I missed all the main veins. He screamed in pain and started breathing deeply to try control it.

I picked up the blow torch and pressed the button, making a blue flame shoot out.

I grinned.

"W-What the fuck are you doing?" He stammered.

"You seem to like tattoos." I observed, he was covered from head to toe in them.

"Y-Yeah."

"I'm a professional, ya know?" I looked at him.

He started to say something but I shushed him. "Don't worry, you're in good hands." I winked and started doing my own version of a tattoo across his chest.

His screams ripped through the room, full of utter agony as the smell of burning flesh filled my nose.

"Okay, okay!" He screamed at the top of his lungs.

I stopped and stepped back, looking at him expectantly.

"You're a fucking psycho." He sobbed.

"Tell us what you know." Chase said lazily.

"Thrash." He said between sobs.

"The President of Thieves Den?" Chase checked.

He nodded.

"What about him?"

"He wants Parker and Heidi. Well, Trigger wants Heidi." He explained, getting weaker and weaker.

I grabbed a shot of adrenaline and injected it into him, making him fully aware again.

"What do they want with the girls?" Chase asked in a hard voice.

"Thrash wants to take Parker from you and Braxton. He knows he can get you to agree to anything if he has her. Trigger loves Heidi, wants her back." He explained in a hurried voice, his eyes looking all around the room.

"Why does he want to negotiate?" Chase growled.

"I don't know." He shook his head. "Thrash and Trig are the only two that know."

"Trigger is scared of me, of the Knights. Why come after Heidi now?"

"Because he's VP now. He has the whole club at his beck and call now."

I shared a look with Chase.

"I'm telling the truth, I swear!" He yelled.

"What else does Thrash want?" Parker walked over, making herself known in the room.

"Parker you shouldn't-" Chase started.

"Why me? Why not just Heidi? She's just as valuable."

He didn't respond.

"Answer her." Chase barked.

"Little girl's shouldn't get involved in a mans world. You're in way over your head, darlin'."

"What are you-" Chase frowned in confusion.

"He wants to take everything." Parker mumbled, shocked.

"What?' Chase and I looked at her.

"I'm the only girl around that's this high up in an MC. I'm a leader, not a whore." She said in a blank voice.

"So?" I shrugged.

"So, Thrash wants to rip that away. He wants to take all my power. He wants to put me in my place.."

"Your place?" Chase said in a hard voice.

"A woman's place is on her knees. Not leading a club." She recited the words she has heard her entire life.

"He wants to make her his woman?" Chase ground out while I stood there, paralyzed by shock and rage.

"Not just his woman.. She'll be passed around the club, then she'll be kept as a whore. Just a sex slave. She won't have a rank or a patch. Thrash will strip her of everything."

"I'm going to fucking slaughter him." My voice was so low and murderous, not even I recognized it.

"He'll never get to her." Chase shook his head fiercely. "To either of them."

"So far his plan is working. Soon enough you'll get a video of all the boys with her and Trig with Heidi."

"Over my dead fucking body." I said, throwing away the blow torch and picking up the chainsaw.

"Fuck! Wait! No!" He screamed, but the sound of the tool drowned him out.

I stared into his eyes as I tore through his leg, cutting it off. Blood pooled everywhere, covering me and squirting all over the place from the severed arteries, the adrenaline shot making him bleed profusely. I quickly did the same to his other leg and laughed as he screamed. I cut the chains loose so he fell on his back to the floor.

Placing my boot on his chest, I did the same to his arms, coating the floor with a thick bloody pool. The life drained from his eyes and I used all my strength to sent the saw into his chest, cutting down until I hit the floor. I tossed it aside and exhaled deeply. I turned around and my eyes locked with Chase, whose face was blank. He was holding Parker, her face buried into his chest. My girl can deal with a lot, but she shouldn't see this.

"Is it over?" She whispered.

"Yeah baby, it's over." I gently touched her back.

She spun around and hugged me, her face in my chest now, her sobs breaking out of her throat like she was choking. I carefully picked her up so she was wrapped around me and I made sure her face was tucked under my chin so she couldn't see the horror movie behind me. The horror movie that I created.

We were all a mess. Chase and Parker from the splash back of blood, and me from being up front and centre. Parker was drenched now from clinging to me and we all quickly left the shed. Chase told Sin and Saint what happened, then clapped my back.

"Get her cleaned up. Make sure none of the wives or kids see you." He told me.

I nodded and walked over to the hose. I placed Parker down and held her up, fearing she couldn't on her own. I turned on the tap and drenched us both, washing off most of the blood. I switched it off and picked her shaking body back up, holding her close.

I walked up to my room and ran a shower, pulling her tank top and jeans off. I left her in her underwear and put her in the hot water. After I quickly stripped down to my briefs, I got in with her and helped her to clean up. She was shaking so bad from shock and she couldn't stop crying.

"Babe." I tipped her chin up to look at me.

"Trust me. I'll protect you. Nothing is going to happen to you on my watch, Princess." I told her firmly.

"I'm scared." She whispered.

She was so vulnerable, so broken and terrified. It broke my heart seeing her like this.

"Don't be scared baby. I won't let anything happen." I promised.

She sobbed and hugged me tightly, clinging to me. I let her cry, soothing her and letting her get it all out until no more tears could fall from her gorgeous green eyes.

I washed her hair for her as best as I could, which, trust me, was not good at all. But at least it was it's normal black colour and not red. Wrapping a towel around her, I sat her down on the floor and I quickly walked off, changing out of the briefs I was wearing and pulling on some track pants. I grabbed a shirt of mine and pulled it over her head, then snapped her bra clip, maneuvering it off of her through the shirt so I didn't see anything. I'm not a total pig.

"Come on, Princess." Lifting her, I placed her in my bed and ran the towel through her hair, then climbed in beside her, holding her smaller frame against my bigger one.

"I love you, Braxton." She breathed as she fell asleep.

I stared down at her with wide eyes. I don't even think she realized she said it. She has never said it out loud before and hearing it filled me with more joy than I could ever explain.

"I love you too, Princess." I mumbled, kissing her hair, knowing she was asleep and couldn't hear the first time I ever admitted it to her.

****

WELL.

That happened.

Don't fuck with Brax, right?

What did you think?

I'm kind of expecting some hate on this chapter really haha, but this is an Action/Romance soooooo :)

But what about the cute stuff at the end?!?!?!

I need to get myself a Braxton hahaha!

Thank you for reading my little chocolate chip cookies! (Yes, that's what I am eating right now, so it was the first thing I thought of)

- Jade xx

Eight Years Later © Khaotik_Angel, 2016

# Chapter Nine:

------------------------------------------------

'C ause girl, I was made for you.

    And girl, you were made for me.

- I was made for loving you - KISS

Chapter Nine:

Parker's P.O.V

I sighed happily and snuggled deeper into the warm body beside me. I haven't slept this comfortable in years. He made a sound in his sleep and turned over, his big arm going around me.

My eyes shot open and I came face to chest with Braxton.

What in the ever loving fuck?!

My heart rate sped up as I tried to recall the events of last night.

Then they came, all in a rush.

I had been inside with Mel and Heidi, watching a stupid reality TV show while the guys all complained. I heard Doug tell Saint that Chase and Brax were with our guest, trying to torture some info out of him for the third day in a row.

Curiosity and boredom got the best of me and I wandered off to the shed. As soon as I stepped in, Braxton was burning our new friends skin with a blow torch. I watched as the skin bubbled and blackened and the sickening smell filled the room.

He eventually spilled about Thrash and Trigger and Braxton went berserk, cutting off all his limbs. After that, everything was a blur. I remember Braxton showering with me, being a perfect gentleman for once in his life, then I remember being carried to his bed. That's it.

I squirmed under Braxton's arm, trying to move him slightly so his arm was still around me, but I wasn't being crushed. He stirred and made a rumbling sound, then pulled me closer in his sleep, crushing my body against his. I wriggled again and then I felt a part of him that was very much awake. We both froze and he made a choked groaning sound as the movement woke him up.

He rolled suddenly so he was hovering over me, my body pinned by his big one. His hair was messy from sleep, but his eyes were sparking blue with lust.

"I-I'm sorry. Your arm was heavy and I was trying to-"

He raised his eyebrow and smirked, cutting off my sentence.

"What?" I scowled.

"You're nervous. You're never nervous." He observed.

"Why would I be nervous?" I demanded.

"Well it could be because you watched me brutally torture and murder someone last night.. But you're used to that.. So it's gotta have something to do with me." He trailed off, pretending to think.

I rolled my eyes.

"It could be that you hate how comfortable you were to be back in my arms.. Or it could be seeing me topless and you were drooling over my perfect physique." He smirked and looked me in the eye. "Or, it could always be this." He rolled his hips slowly, pressing his hard length against the thin fabric of my lace underwear. I instinctively clutched his biceps and moaned, fluttering my eyes closed.

"Yeah, I think that's it." He whispered against my neck, kissing it gently and rolling his hips again, forming a perfect grove in my panties. I moaned as he throbbed against me and he caught the skin of my neck between his teeth, biting me, hard. I clutched his arms tighter and my breaths turned into erratic little moans.

His lips traveled up to my mouth and he kissed me deeply, our tongues twisting together. I slowly spread my legs apart, giving him better access and his hands grabbed my legs, pulling them up to wrap around his waist.

"Argh, Brax." I whimpered as he teased me.

"What do you want baby girl?" He mumbled, his voice so deep and sexy as he sucked on my neck.

"I want you to make me come." I breathed, pulling his face back to mine so I could kiss his lips again. He groaned at my words and traced his hands over my body, slowly, caressing me. He sat up on his knees and pulled his shirt off of my body, leaving me in nothing but my panties, which he then slowly slid off of my legs. He kept hold of my legs and he placed my feet on either of his shoulders.

"Holy fuck." He groaned, looking down at my naked body.

"Brax." I reached out for him and he smirked, kissing one of my legs. He worked his lips up the inside of my leg at an agonizingly slow pace. When his face was on his inside of my thigh, he looked up at me and I almost came right there, seeing his blue eyes shinning. His hot tongue flicked out and I cried out, fisting my hands in the sheets.

"God damn Park, you taste fucking incredible." He groaned before running his tongue along me again. He was so talented with his tongue, running it up and down my clit, then poking it inside of me to the point where I was on the verge of having one of the most intense orgasms of my life. My moans were loud and desperate as I ran my fingers through his hair, gripping it as I felt myself on the edge.

"Come for me, Princess." He mumbled against me, the words and the vibration of his deep voice was my undoing and I screamed out his name incoherently, riding out the waves of my orgasm as he lapped up everything I gave him. When he was satisfied that he had cleaned me up, he lifted his head and his eyes went to my hip, where his name proudly sat. He kissed over the ink and then kissed me on the mouth, slower than before, sweetly. I felt him against my thigh, hard as a rock and I ran my hand down his chest, going to grab him through his pants. He caught my hand and brought it back up to his chest and looked at me.

"This is about you. Not me." He told me.

"But you-"

"Baby, I'll be fine." He interrupted me and kissed the tip of my nose. "God, I've wanted to do that for years." He groaned, licking his lips. "I could do that all day just to watch you come and hear you scream my name." He winked and smirked at me.

"Shut up." I laughed and rolled my eyes at him.

He chuckled and looked into my eyes with a smile, his eyes full of emotion.

"What?" I tilted my head to the side.

He shook his head and kissed me quickly. "Nothing, you're just incredible. And gorgeous." He looked down at my naked body.

I ran my hand through his hair and then my stomach growled loudly, ruining the moment completely.

"Hungry?" He laughed.

"I didn't eat last night." I nodded.

"Come on." He got to his feet and pulled me up with him, pushing his shirt back on my body.

"I'll meet you down there." I got on my tiptoes and kissed the edge of his jaw before running out and making my way to my own room. I threw the shirt on my bed and got in the shower, washing my body and my hair, then I stepped out, pulling on a pair of denim shorts and a black top that hung off one shoulder. I went to grab my cut, but it wasn't where I left it. I shrugged, throwing my gun and knife in my shorts and skipped downstairs, going into the kitchen. Braxton, Chase, Sin, Saint, Heidi and Mel were all in there. The boys at the table, laughing and the two girls in the kitchen, talking.

"Damn Parker, looking good." Doug came up behind me and grabbed my hand, spinning me in a circle.

I narrowed my eyes at him.

"It's a compliment girl, geez." He laughed.

"Don't mind him, you look gorgeous." Mel winked at me.

I blew her a kiss went over to the guys, sitting beside Brax.

"What's new?" I asked casually.

"The girls are cooking breakfast." Saint grinned.

"You doing okay?" Chase asked me.

"I'm fine." I shrugged.

"Good. I need you to be strong right now. For the boys and.." He trailed off and looked at Heidi.

"For fuck sake man, just make her your woman already." Saint pushed his shoulder.

"Shut the fuck up before I shove my foot so deep up your ass that you cough up my boot." Chase ground out.

"Defensive." I sang with a smirk.

"Parker I swear to fucking-"

"Have you heard from Jesse since the other day?" Heidi interrupted him unknowingly and collapsed in my lap.

"I honestly don't know. Seems like forever ago, I haven't even checked my phone." I admitted.

"Poor kid." She laughed. "Parker the heart breaker."

I rolled my eyes.

"Hey guys." Candy and another one of the club whores, Lola, walked in.

"Ladies." Saint and Doug grinned at them.

"Hardly." Heidi muttered, making me laugh.

Mel set down a huge plate of food and slid into the chair beside me.

"Thanks Mel." I kissed her cheek and we all dug into the food. Heidi demolished her food while she sat on my lap and I tried to maneuver around her, devouring my egg and bacon sandwich.

"I need to go back home. I need my computer and textbooks. I really need to study." Mel groaned as we all finished.

"I'll take you." Sin and Doug said at the same time, then glared at each other.

"You have stuff to do here today." I told Doug.

"Oh yeah? Whats that?" He looked at me, knowing I was making it up.

"Wash my bike." Brax told him.

"What?" Doug looked at him blankly.

"My bike needs to be washed." He shrugged.

"Seriously?" Doug looked at me.

"Sorry Doug." I smiled and he got up, stomping off.

"Come on, gorgeous." Sin stood up and winked at her.

"Will.. It be okay?" She looked from Sin, to me, to Chase.

"You'll be safe." I promised her.

"Trust me babe, I won't let anything happen to you." He smiled.

"Okay." She nodded and got up, following him out.

Chase got up too and stretched, going to walk away.

"Where are you going?" Candy jumped up and touched his chest.

"Uh.. To shower." He said like it was a question.

"Want company?" She looked up at him.

"I'll pass." He laughed and pushed her hand away, walking off.

"Thought I told you to stay away from him." Heidi said in a hard voice.

"Who are you to tell me that? Chase is open season honey." Candy laughed.

"No, he's not." She ground between her teeth.

"Aw, does little Heidi have a crush on the boss?" Candy patronized her.

She jumped up and glared at her. "Fuck you."

"You're just a fuck to him, you know that right." Lola tuned in.

"Well, while he's fucking me, he isn't fucking any of you dirty hoes."

"Guys, chill out." I sighed and stood up behind Heidi.

"That an order?" Candy smirked.

"You want it to be?" I narrowed my eyes at her.

"You can't just tell us we aren't allowed to sleep with certain guys. Unless they have an old lady, they're free." She shrugged.

"Like Brax." Candy looked at him as I stepped around Heidi.

"Don't even go there." I glared at her.

"You aren't so high and mighty, Parker. Chase is the boss. You're just his little slut of a sister."

I snapped my fist into her face and sent her back into the floor as blood pissed out of her nose.

"Listen to me you little hooker. I'm a fucking Greyson. My used tampons are worth more than your entire life. I've earned my place and if I order you to stay away from Chase, you stay the fuck away from Chase. If I order you to keep your legs closed around my man. You'll fucking do it. or I'll make you wish you never heard of the Knights. Got it?" I cocked my head to the side.

She looked away from me, tears welling in her eyes. I picked her up by her arm and spun her so her was bent over the cupboard, with me gripping her hair.

"Are. We fucking. Clear?"

"Y-Yes."

"Yes what?"

"Yes Parker. Yes boss."

"Who are you staying away from?"

"Chase and Braxton." She sobbed.

"This is your last warning sweetheart. Next time, the only thing you get shoved up you will be my fucking gun." I threw her aside and she fell to the floor in a heap.

"Out." I looked at Lola, who was sitting in Saint's lap. She jumped up and grabbed Candy, leading her out.

"Parker, for fuck sake." Saint groaned, annoyed I just scared away his next fuck.

"Girl, you can be plain scary at times." Heidi shook her head, instead of looking pissed off like I expected, she looked sad.

"Hey, don't take it to heart." I cocked my head at her.

"Yeah, yeah." She sniffed and ran her hand across her eyes.

"Heidi they are just jealous that you have Chase's attention."

"Ugh, why the fuck am I even crying?" She growled. "I'm fine." She sighed and walked off.

Saint got up too and grumbled to himself as he grabbed the last piece of toast and left the room, leaving me with a grinning Braxton.

"What are you so smiley about?" I frowned, sitting back down beside him.

"Your man huh?" His grin widened.

I frowned and then it clicked. I groaned.

"I like that. It's only fair, you are my girl after all." He pulled me into his lap so I was straddling him and he kissed me deeply. "You're fucking hot when you're jealous." He continued, his hands on my behind, holding me against him.

"I catch you with one of those sluts, and I'll be your worst nightmare." I mumbled against his mouth.

"I know. You're a fucking psycho and I love it." He bit my lip hard, making me melt into him.

****

Pheww, a sexy scene with Brax and Parker *fans self*

What did you think of this chapter?

What about Heidi and Chase?

Thank you so much for reading my little potatoes!

- Jade xx

Eight Years Later © Khaotik_Angel, 2016

# Chapter Ten:

------------------------------------------------

I'm only half here, if my girl's not.

- Home Is Where The Heart Is - Bliss and Eso

Chapter Ten:

Parker's P.O.V

I let out a slow breath and pressed the trigger, one shot after another, all hitting the target at the end of the range. Two in the heart, one in the dick and two in the head. I pulled back and changed clips, cracking my neck as I cocked the gun and a new target appeared.

"Ugh!" Heidi yelled, making me jump and miss my shot. I sighed and placed the gun down, turning to glare at her.

"You need to relax more, babe." Chase mumbled. He was standing directly behind her, his hands on her hips.

"I am relaxed. Can't I just skip out? I'm starving!" She yelled.

"You just ate!" Chase laughed and then sighed, "Here." He took the handgun and calmly reloaded it, handing it back to her. "Legs spread." He moved his hands to move her legs shoulder width apart. "Arms out." He moved her arms ahead of her, stretched out.

"Now, you need to hold the gun tightly. Keep your arms straight and focus your muscle. If you don't, the gun will kick back."

I grinned at the two of them and kept watching in silence.

"Like this?" Heidi looked at him.

"Good girl. Now, look at your target and line up your shot." He leaned down so he was at her height and helped her line up the target.

"Deep breath in."

She did as he said, slowly.

"Now, slowly let it out, as you do, hit the trigger."

She exhaled and pressed the trigger, sending a bullet into the heart of the target.

"I did it!" She screamed, placing the gun down and turning to jump on Chase, wrapping her legs around his waist.

"Good job babe." He laughed and held her to him, kissing her deeply.

The were honestly adorable.

I peaked over at Brax, who was shooting the targets at ease, like a pro. He wore a white tank top and dark jeans with his cut on and motorcycle boots. I watched as he expertly reloaded the gun in record time and shot at some more targets. He looked bored.

"Sin, you crazy motherfucker." Saint muttered from the door.

"Huh?" I turned towards him.

Saint looked over at us and nodded his head outside. We all walked over, out curiosity peaked. Sin was sat on his Harley with Mel straddling him, her arms around his neck as he kissed her. Sin kissed her with such care, being so gentle with her and Mel looked like she was in heaven, melting right into his muscled chest. Something must of happened between them when he took her to get her things yesterday, they have been inseparable ever since. They had obviously spoken about the situation, unlike my giant chicken of a best friend who still hadn't spoken to Chase.

"Melanie!" Doug's voice cut through the moment as he stormed over.

"Doug!" She scrambled to get off the bike but Sin kept a firm grip on her as he evenly looked at her brother.

"Get the fuck off my baby sister." He growled.

"Doug, bro." Sin sighed and lifted Mel off the bike as he climbed off too.

"I'm sick of trying to hide it. It's not fair to you, or me and Mel." Sin started.

"What does that mean?" Doug narrowed his eyes.

"I've always cared about you Mel. We have always had.. Something. As much as I tried to snuff it out, I can't get you out of my head. I know you deserve better than the life I live.. But I would always protect you, I'd give my life for you in a heartbeat." He looked at his twin brother, seeing all of us there, then back at Mel.

"Holy mother of fuck, is he..?" Heidi trailed off.

"The Knights are my family. Chase isn't just my boss.. My president. He's my brother. Brax, Saint, all the guys.. Doug." He stopped to look at Doug. "I love these guys. We're a brother hood. Park and Heidi, they're my family too. I've known them since we were teenagers and they are my sisters. I'd take a bullet for anyone on this compound. We're bikers.. But we're a family." He took a deep breath and reached into the bag on his Harley, pulling out a black box with a pink ribbon.

"Mel, I want you to be in that family. I want you by my side. I want you to be my old lady."

"Holy shit." I mumbled, throwing my hand out to whack Heidi, who was to shocked to even feel it.

Mel sniffed and gently took the box, opening it. We all leaned forward, trying to see inside, but we were way to far away to even have a hope in hell.

Mel pulled the leather cut out and looked it over, then jumped into Sin's arms, taking him by surprise. He caught her and stumbled back a step, laughing.

"That a yes?" He asked.

"Of course it is you idiot! It took you long enough!" She cried out.

He laughed and put her down, holding out the cut. She slid it on over her jeans and purple T-shirt. The club patch stood out on the back and stitched on the breast were the words "Sin's girl"

Mel turned around and kissed him, her happy tears mixing into the kiss as she clung to him. Even in the kiss, Sin's grin was huge.

I snuck a look at Doug to see him in total shock, mouth hanging open and his eyes bugging out of their sockets.

"Did you know about this?" I looked at Chase.

"He made me swear to not tell a soul." Chase chuckled.

"I'm so happy for them!" Heidi squeaked. Chase looked down at her, with a look of longing in his eyes. He wanted that. How could he not see that she did too?

Hell, even I wanted that. I wanted Brax's name stitched into my own cut.

Hoots and cheers rang out across the yard from the other brothers and Sin grinned, looking at them all. Mel hid in his chest and then ran over to us as Sin went over to Doug.

"Let me see!" Heidi held her at arms length and examined the cut, then pulled her into a huge hug.

Mel looked at me and walked over, her huge blue eyes sparkling.

"Congratulations honey." I hugged her tight then pulled back and brushed her hair behind her ear. "Welcome to the family."

New tears ran down her cheeks and she hugged me again. Next, she looked at Chase, looking a little wary.

"Welcome to the Knights." He smiled and kissed her cheek.

"Thank you Chase.. So much." She hugged him and he stroked her hair back.

"Who would've thought a little blonde haired, blue eyed nurse could tame my brother." Saint laughed.

"Shut up." She scowled at him adorably and he picked her up into a bear hug.

"Congratulations love." Braxton hugged her as well.

"Look." Heidi gasped. We all looked over to see Sin and Doug hugging.

"Bout time." Saint mumbled.

The two men walked over and Mel ran to her brother, hugging him tightly and talking to him away from us.

"I'm proud of you, bro." Saint hugged his brother.

"Thanks man." He laughed, then looked at Heidi and I.

"Who knew you would be sweet?" I smirked.

"I'm not." He narrowed his eyes at me.

"You are! That was so cute. You did well Sin." Heidi hugged him and he kissed the top of her head, then looked at me. "Come on Park, we all know you aren't that heartless." He rolled his eyes.

"Oh, but I am." I poked my tongue out at him.

"Come here you feisty pain in my ass." He laughed and picked me up into a hug. I laughed and hugged him back.

"You did well. I'm happy for you." I told him as he put me down.

"Yeah, congratulations brother." Braxton hugged him.

"You two next, yeah?" Sin smirked at Brax and Chase.

"Something like that." Chase mumbled, his eyes locked on Heidi, whose eyes bugged at the comment. He hugged Sin and Brax looked at me the same was Chase looked at Heidi, with longing.

The same look in my eyes when I looked at him.

****

I knowww, this is a much shorter chapter! DON'T ATTACK ME!

What did you guys think of all the vomit-worthy cute moments in this chapter?!?!

Sin and Mel are now official!! Yayyyyy!! :)

Thank you so much for reading my little poodle puffs!

- Jade xx

Eight Years Later © Khaotik_Angel, 2016

# Chapter Eleven:

My terror twin and I,

Let's take over the world

- Someone, Somewhere - Asking Alexandria

Chapter Eleven:

Parker's P.O.V

I looked around Sin's room with a satisfied face. Mel had really done a number on this place. Heidi, Mel and I had been working all week and Mel had demanded that Sin needed to replace his bed if she was going to live there, so it wasn't a constant question if how many women had already been in it. We had cleaned the carpet so it looked brand new with no stains. She had placed her desk in the room with all her studying stuff and the room now looked welcoming. When your on lock down, there really is nothing else to do so we had thrown ourselves into getting her settled.

"Sin is going to flip." Heidi laughed.

"He sure is." Mel grinned.

"Long as you're happy babe." Sin walking in then and picked her up into his arms, kissing her deeply. She giggled against his mouth and wrapped her legs around his waist. It started getting a little heated and I looked at Heidi.

"Get out." Sin said to us against Mel's mouth.

"Don't be rude!" She pulled back and slapped his chest slightly.

"Fine." He rolled his eyes and looked at us. "Unless you want to watch me fuck Mel on this bed, I would suggest leaving."

"Sin!" Mel laughed.

"Gross." I shuddered, grabbed Heidi's hand and pulled her out the room with me, slamming the door shut.

"Lock down is so boring." She sighed as we walked downstairs. I jumped on her back and she stumbled in surprise before regaining her balance.

"God, fat ass." She groaned as we walked into the kitchen and grabbed a pile of snacks.

"Fat? Please, I'm not the one who just grabbed enough food to feed an army." I laughed as she walked into the lounge room.

Chase and Brax looked up from where they were sitting on the couch, watching American Chopper with a beer in hand.

"You are fat. And I'm starving." Heidi grumbled, dumping all the food on the table.

"Don't hate on me, we both know I have killer curves. You're always hungry." I pulled at her hair and she pushed me off her so dropped to the floor.

"Ow!" I groaned as she bent over laughing.

"You're such a cow." I booted her in her giant ass and she tumbled forward.

"Oh it's on." She turned to glare at me.

I jumped up and put my fists up in front of my face playfully.

"Must you two do that in here?" Chase sighed.

"We must!" Heidi threw her arms in the air dramatically. "Chasey I'm bored!"

"Chasey, me too!" I joined in, pouting.

He threw his head back and groaned in annoyance.

"C'mon Chasey!" Heidi poked him in the chest.

I jumped on the couch, landing on both the men, my head at Braxton's end.

"We're bored!" I exclaimed.

"Well find something to do." Chase sighed.

"Okay." Heidi shrugged and went to leave the room.

"Well that was easy." Chase mumbled.

Heidi stopped at the door and turned to Chase.

"I'll be in your room, kay? Up to you if you want to join me." She smirked then strutted out.

"Slut!" I called after her.

"I learn from the best!" I heard her yell back.

"I'm out." Chase jumped up, chugged his beer then practically ran out of the room.

"So gross." I muttered.

"That means I need to keep you entertained now, doesn't it?" Braxton sighed.

"Sure does!" I jumped up so I was on my knees beside him.

"What do you wanna do, Princess?" He chuckled and looked at me.

I shrugged, "wanna go for a ride?"

"We're on lock down." He smirked.

"What can I say? I'm a bad girl." I winked and jumped up.

His eyes skimmed over my dark jeans and white crop top. "Okay."

I grinned and ran upstairs, throwing on my motorcycle boots and going to grab my leather cut. I frowned into my wardrobe and ripped through it.

"What are you doing?" Braxton asked as he came in.

"I can't find my cut." I mumbled.

"Is it in the bathroom?" He asked.

I checked and came back out, shaking my head.

"It'll turn up babe. Come on. Make sure you're packing." He said, pushing his gun into his jeans.

I sighed and pulled on a denim jacket and pushed my weapons inside. We walked down to the garage and Braxton tied a bandana around his face, climbing on his bike and kick starting it, making the engine roar to life. he held out a sleek black helmet and I pushed it on, jumping on behind him. I rested my hands on his abs and positioned myself so I was pressed against him.

"Remind me to take you on my bike more often." He mumbled in a husky voice.

"Just drive, stud." I laughed, making him chuckle and pull out of the compound, speeding down the road. The engine was so chunky and loud as he drove down the roads. It wasn't until we started winding through the hills that I realized where he was taking me. To our spot.

When we got there, Braxton climbed off and looked at me. I pulled the helmet off and put it down as I jumped up and walked over to see the view. It was sunset and the sky was a gorgeous shade of pinks, purples and oranges.

"God, I love it here." I mumbled as a light breeze lifted my hair.

"Me too." Braxton stood beside me and we watched the busy city below us in silence.

"Are you worried?" I looked at him.

"About?" He turned to me.

"Thieves Den."

"I think I would be a bad VP if I wasn't worried. Every threat is a threat, no matter how much I believe we will kick their ass. The club is still in danger, so that worries me." He mumbled.

"So profound." I teased him.

He laughed and threw his arm over my shoulders, bringing me into his chest.

"That being said, if our intel is right, we have twice as many guys than Thieves Den. They would be idiots to attack us."

"Heidi is scared. She doesn't show it as much, but she's scared of Trigger." I looked out at the view, the sun almost gone now.

"And you?" He asked.

"Me?" I raised an eyebrow.

"Are you scared of Thrash?"

I thought about that for a second, then looked at him. "I think I'd be a bad leader if I wasn't worried. Every threat is a threat, no matter how much I believe we will kick their ass. The club, my family, is in danger, so that worries me." I repeated his words.

He nodded and kissed my lips gently. I leaned into him and kissed him back, placing my hand on his bicep to steady me. He nipped at my lip and I opened my mouth, giving him access to twist his tongue with mine. I moaned into his mouth and bit his tongue gently. I quickly got up and climbed into his lap, straddling him without breaking the kiss and he pressed his hands down on my hips. I moved my lips down and ran my teeth over his neck, sucking down as I held his big arms.

"Fuck, Parker." He moaned, pulling off my jacket and tossing it aside. I pushed his cut off and tore his shirt off of his body, then kissed his mouth again, running my hands down his chest. It was like a fire was ignited within me every time he touched me.

He gripped my top and slowly pulled it off, kissing down my neck and moving my bra aside to take my nipple in his mouth. I gasped and tipped my head back as his tongue swirled around and he sucked gently. I moaned loudly and rocked my body against him, needing friction, needing contact. Just needing him.

His hands went to the front of my jeans and he unbuttoned them as I stood up to take them off, leaving me in my underwear set. Brax yanked his pants off and grabbed a foil packet out his pocket, pulling me back down to him.

He flipped us over so my back was protected from the grass by his cut then he kissed me again. His hands ran down my body and he slowly pulled down my panties, then spread my legs wide. I whimpered and clutched his briefs, making him chuckle and take them off, pushing the condom on. Brax got on his knees and placed his tip at my entrance, making me moan with want.

"Braxton, please." I panted.

He smirked and rolled his hips, pushing into me a few inches, as a loud cry left my throat.

"Fuck Parker, you're so tight." He groaned.

"More." I begged as he pushed inside me more, until I had his full length. I felt my body stretch to accommodate him and I loved the pain it shot through me. He started to move and I couldn't control all the desperate moans that left me as he slowly moved in and out of me.

"Harder." I breathed.

He grunted and hooked his hands under my knees, wrapping them around his waist as he lowered himself down to me and pushed into me, hard and fast. I screamed out and clutched his arms as he increased the pace, fucking me like I had always wanted him to. His lips went to my neck and he sucked my flesh as he pumped me, building me higher and higher up.

"Oh God, Braxton, I'm gonna- I-"

"Fucking drown me, babe." He said into my ear, his voice sending jolts through me.

"Oh Jesus fucking Christ!" I screamed out as he bit down on my shoulder so hard I knew it would leave marks. I hope it did. I screamed out long and loud as I came, clinging to him for dear life as he continued to thrust inside me. He was moaning and cursing under his breath at my release and I quickly flipped us so I was on top of him. He looked up at me and placed his hands on my hips. I rocked my hips and he clenched his jaw, making a strangled noise. I placed my hands on his hard arms and increased my pace until I was really riding him. Every thrust hit my sweet spot and I felt myself come apart again, screaming out his name.

"Holy shit, Parker. Fuck!" He yelled, his hands clenching on my hips, holding me down as his dick throbbed and then exploded into the condom. I moaned at the feeling and slowed down, then stopped, collapsing on his chest. Both of our hearts were racing and our breathing was hard and fast.

"Fucking hell." He mumbled after a few minutes.

I moved my head to look up at him.

"That was.. Fucking amazing. Better than I ever thought." He panted.

I nodded in agreement.

"Come here." He pulled my chin up and he kissed me, softly, lazily. I sighed in pure bliss and cuddled into him.

"We should go." He sighed, clearly not wanting to.

"Yeah." I nuzzled his neck, then got to my feet, wincing as I stood up fully. I pulled on my clothes and watched as Brax did the same, tying up the condom and tossing it away. He pulled me into his arms and held me for awhile, my eyes fluttering closed. Braxton's phone rang and he pulled it from his pocket, pressing it to his ear.

"Yeah?"

"Get here right fucking now!" I could hear Chase yell into the phone. "We've been attacked bro."

"Fuck. I'm there." Brax barked, then hung up, both of us going to his bike. He kick started it as I threw the helmet on and I held onto him as he basically flew back to the compound.

He pulled into the drive way and I heard him curse. I looked around him and gasped. I threw the helmet off, and we both got off the bike, pulling out our guns.

Fuck.

****

Mwahahahahaha! What do you guys think could be going on?!

What about the scene with Braxton and Parker?! ;)

Thank you so much for reading my little munchies!

- Jade xx

Eight Years Later © Khaotik_Angel, 2016

# Chapter Twelve:

----

D anger's part of what we do.

- Hell On Wheels - Brantley Gilbert

** Quick note before we begin! I have added short lyrics to the beginning of each chapter, like this one ^ They relate to either; the character/the upcoming chapter/the relationship between two characters/a situation/or just something I think fits :) Feel free to have a quick look back and tell me your thoughts! They are super short and I'd appreciate it! Do you know any of the songs? Which ones do you feel relate the most? **

Thanks guys! Now, chapter twelve!

Chapter Twelve:

Parker's P.O.V

"What the fuck happened?" Braxton asked Chase as I looked around at all the scattered dead bodies littering the front of the compound.

"The fuckers got into the property! Thieves-mother-fucking-Den. They killed all the security and the guards and were leaving before any of us made it outside." Chase was fuming, his eyes blazing with fury.

"Any of the main brothers?" I swallowed as sadness crossed Chase's face.

"Oh God, who?" I gasped.

"It's Doug.. He ran out first, ahead of us and got shot in the thigh."

"Is he alive?" I clutched Braxton's arm for support.

"Mel's working on him now."

I ran inside and Chase led me over to the lounge room where Doug was lying on the couch, a bottle of vodka in his hand. Heidi clutched his other hand as Mel worked on her brother, Sin stood back, watching Mel carefully.

"Jesus Christ." I mumbled, coming closer.

"Park?" Doug ground out.

"The one and only." I said lightly, standing beside Heidi, clutching the same hand.

"They got me." He mumbled.

"It's just a flesh wound, don't be a baby." I teased.

He laughed, then sucked in a breath as it shot pain through his body.

"I need help." Mel whispered.

"What do you need, love?" Chase said from behind me.

"The bullet is the only thing plugging the hole, as soon as I take it out, I need you to press this into the hole." She held up some gauze.

"No problem." Chase rounded the couch and grabbed it from her.

"Parker, cut his jeans, Heidi, hold this down, hard." Mel ordered, nodding to where she was holding down a shirt, her hands covered in blood.

"I-I-" Heidi shook her head from side to side.

"Heidi?" Mel looked up at her.

"I can't- The blood." Heidi stumbled back.

"What are you doing? Since when does blood bother you?" I turned to look at my ghost white best friend.

"I'm sorry." She breathed, then gagged and ran out of the room.

"I got it." Brax moved and held down the shirt. Sin handed me scissors and I cut off Doug's jeans so the wound was exposed.

"Hold on!" Doug quickly drank more of the vodka, breathing deeply.

"Ready?" Mel looked at Brax, who nodded.

Brax pulled the shirt away and Mel used a tool dig into Doug's leg and pull the bullet out.

"Fuck!" He yelled, grabbing my hand and squeezing.

"It's okay, it's okay." I pushed his hair back and soothed him while Mel poured vodka in the hole and Chase pushed the gauze into his leg.

"There, it's okay." I kissed his head gently.

Chase said something to Brax, then ran out the room, probably after Heidi.

"Good job brother." Brax told Doug.

"I'll fucking kill that cunt." He grit out.

"Trust me, you'll get revenge." Braxton muttered darkly.

I stayed with Doug and Mel while the others left later on.

"You doing okay?" I looked at her.

"If I wasn't here.." She trailed off.

"You did an incredible job, Mel. You worked amazingly well under pressure." I hugged her as we watched Doug sleep.

"I'm not even a full nurse yet, Park. I don't graduate till the end of this year."

"Based on this, you'll graduate with flying colours." I squeezed her.

"Hey baby, come on let's get you to bed." Sin came in and looked at Mel.

"I can't leave him." She shook her head.

"Then we will sleep in here. You need sleep, babe." He pleaded.

"Sin's right. Get some sleep, love." I kissed her head and stood up.

"Boys wanna see you." Sin told me as I went to leave. I nodded and walked up to Chase's office. Brax, Chase, Heidi and Saint all sat there.

"What's up?" I asked, closing the door.

"I choked." Heidi suddenly sobbed, bursting into tears. She ran over to me and clutched onto me for dear life.

I stumbled a little, taken off guard and I looked at Chase, who looked at her like he was just as confused and clueless as me.

"Hey, it's okay. Doug will be fine." I soothed her.

"I fucked up! I couldn't do it! The blood-" She cut off and held back a gag.

"Heidi, sit down." I walked her over to the table and sat her down, but she refused to let go of me.

"Babe, what's up?" I pushed her hair out of her face and sat on the table.

"It made me squeamish." She mumbled.

"But you've never been squeamish before." I frowned in confusion.

"I don't know!" She sobbed and cried into her hands.

"Babe just-" Chase started.

"Shut the fuck up, Chase!" She jumped up and screamed at him.

"Heidi-"

"No, fuck you! I'm so sick of you playing me! I'm not a fucking sex puppet, you asshole!" She screamed, then ran out the office.

"Christ, what did you do?" I breathed, looking at a shocked Chase.

"I have no fucking idea." He mumbled, staring at the door.

I shook my head and sat at the table.

"To business." Chase cleared his throat. "The Den have gone way to far this time. Killing all the security and guards and then shooting Doug is not going to be tolerated. I'm waging war." He stared straight into my eyes.

"Good idea. We need to teach them they can't fuck with the Knights." I nodded.

"Boys?" Chase looked at Saint and Brax.

"Let's do this." Saint grinned.

"I'm in." Brax agreed.

"Good. How do we retaliate for now?" Chase looked at us all.

"The Den get their guns by a shipment at the dock. We could hijack it." Brax suggested.

"They also have a meth dealer a couple towns over. Could blow the lab." Saint added.

"Parker?" Chase looked at me.

"Shipment will be full of AK's. They would come in handy in a war." I looked at him.

"Shipment it is." Chase hit the gavel on the table and we all relaxed back.

"How's Mel?" Saint asked.

"Shaken up and worried. She'll be okay. She's sleeping in there with Sin tonight, doesn't wanna leave Doug." I explained.

He nodded.

"So you have no idea what's up with Heidi?" Chase leaned forward.

"No idea." I frowned.

"Girl's been having crazy mood swings lately." He sighed.

"Probably her period." I shrugged.

"No, it's not that. She hasn't had one in awhile cause when she does she steers clear of me." Chase mumbled.

"What?" My eyes popped open and I looked at my brother.

"What?" He frowned at me.

"Chase.." I trailed off.

"What?" All three men looked at me with confusion.

"What happens when a girl skips her period?" I raised my eyebrows, willing him to understand.

"Means she's-" He froze.

"Fuck." Saint mumbled in shock.

"No.." Chase shook his head lightly. "I wrap my shit up."

"She needs a test. Now." I jumped up.

"Fuck!" He yelled, slamming his fist into the table.

"Keep him here." I looked at Brax, who was just as dumbstruck. He nodded and I ran up to Heidi's room, opening the door.

"Heidi?" I called out.

I was answered by the sound of her puking in her bathroom and I quickly shut the door and ran inside to hold her hair back.

"Parker." She whimpered, tears mixing with the vomit.

"Shh, it's okay." I rubbed her back.

When she was done and had had a shower, she came out and sat on her bed.

"I have an idea of what could be up." I mumbled.

"Don't say it." She whispered.

I held up a pregnancy test.

"No, Parker." She sobbed.

"You've taken one?" My eyebrows shot up.

"No. I'm avoiding taking one. Chase will hate me. He'll kick me out." She cried.

"The hell he will. Come on hun. I'm right here." I handed it to her and she took a shaky breath and looked at me.

"I love you." I smiled.

"Love you too." She sniffed and walked into the bathroom again.

"You gotta wait three minutes!" I called to her.

She paced around the room as we waited and when her phone buzzed, she gulped and walked over to the white stick, picking it up.

"Pregnant." She whispered, fresh tears pooling in her eyes.

****

What do you think of this chapter?

Are you shocked by Heidi's news?!

Thank you so much for reading my little cupcakes!

If you're enjoying this story, feel free to vote/comment and follow me, it would mean a lot! :)

- Jade xx

Eight Years Later © Khaotik_Angel, 2016

# Chapter Thirteen:

------------------------------------------------

A nd I know I'm right

For the first time in my life.

- Better Be Home Soon - Crowded House

Chapter Thirteen:

Parker's P.O.V

I chewed on my lip, waiting for Chase and Heidi to get back from the doctors office while Braxton stood behind me, his arms around my front and his face nuzzled into my neck.

"Stop worrying." He kissed behind my ear gently.

"Chase better not be a jerk about this." I mumbled.

"If he is I'll hold him down while you beat the shit out of him." He chuckled. "He won't be, babe. He will be in shock for awhile but he'll be happy. It's with Heidi after all."

"Anything yet?" Saint walked out and lit up a cigarette.

"Nope." I took a deep breath and let it out slowly.

"He won't walk out, Park." Saint smiled.

"How do you know?" I sighed.

"He's twenty nine, Park. We aren't teenagers anymore. Chase has the MC, he has the money and the mansion. He has you and he has Heidi. Why wouldn't he be excited to start a family?" Saint shrugged. "I mean, fuck. If I had a girl right now, I'd knock her up as soon as I get my patch on her." He chuckled.

"Really?" I raised my eyebrows in surprise.

"Yeah. There are no guarantees in this life. I could die tomorrow or in twenty years from now. Why wait? I'd kill to have what Chase is about to have." He blew out a cloud of smoke and looked at me. "Plus, now, Sin's got Mel. Brax has you.." He trailed off and shrugged.

"You'll find her, man. Takes a special girl to be with a guy like us." Braxton told him. "But, trust me. It's worth the wait." He finished, squeezing me tighter against him.

"Sin told me your story last night." Mel tuned in, rounding the corner, smiling at me.

"He did?" I raised my eyebrow.

"Yeah, why didn't you ever tell me?" She cocked her head, sadly.

"Not something I like going into." I shrugged.

"Why?" She frowned lightly.

"Imagine Sin being taken to jail for eight years right now." I looked at her as watched as her face showed heartbreak and pain. "That's why." I mumbled, looking away.

"I'm sorry, Park."

"It's fine. How's Doug?" I asked as Braxton kissed my shoulder gently.

"He's sleeping. I'm giving him something for the pain and it's helping him. But he won't be able to walk for awhile."

I nodded and she walked off.

"So what is your deal now?" Saint cocked his head to the side, staring between me and Braxton.

Neither of us said anything for a minute.

"I'm waiting until she stops being stubborn." Braxton finally said, kissing my cheek.

Saint looked at me.

"I'm waiting for him to man up and ask me." I smirked.

"What?" Braxton spun me around so he was looking at me.

I winked at him and his jaw dropped.

"But- You-I-" He stuttered.

The front door opened and I turned quickly to see Heidi and Chase walk in.

"How did it go?" I asked, stepping forward.

"We're having a baby." Chase announced, pulling Heidi into his side and kissing her head.

"For real?!" I shouted.

"Yes, Park, for real." He rolled his eyes.

I screamed and ran to him, jumping on him. He caught me and hugged me tightly. He put me down and I hugged Heidi as Braxton pulled Chase into a hug. Saint came over as well and I placed my hands on Heidi's tummy, it was still flat, but had a little hard bulge.

"How far along?" I asked, my eyes bugging.

"Just hit three months." Heidi mumbled.

"Three months?!" My jaw dropped.

"Yeah, I didn't even realize. The symptoms only started recently." She shrugged.

"What about the alcohol and all that?" I stood up straight.

"I told the doctor and she said the baby looks to be in perfect health, so it should be fine as long as I don't have another drink through the pregnancy." Heidi rubbed her tummy.

"I can't believe you're having a baby." I sniffed and hugged my best friend.

"Neither can I." She laughed and hugged me back.

"So, you like the sound of Aunty Parker?" Chase asked.

"I love it." I laughed and wiped away my tears.

"This place definitely needs to make some changes if there's going to be a little baby around." Heidi smiled, pulling back.

"I agree. But first things first.." Chase grinned and looked at Braxton, who grinned and jogged off, coming back a few seconds later with a box.

"Thought it was about time I did this." Chase laughed and reached into the box, pulling out Heidi's leather cut.

"Chase." She breathed, her hands going to her mouth.

"You know how much you mean to me Heids. In my mind, you've always been my girl. I was just to stubborn to admit it. Seems to run in the family." He stopped to give me a look. "Anyway. You're my sisters best friend. You're a sister to the boys here. You're already family. On top of that, you've got my baby and there's no one I'd rather go through this with. So, be my girl? Wear my patch?" Chase smirked.

"I can't believe it took my getting pregnant for you to do this." She laughed and wiped her eyes. "Yes." She nodded and he scooped her up in a huge hug, kissing her deeply. The three of us cheered and I heard a few other eavesdroppers start cheering as well. Chase helped Heidi into her cut and she looked down at the new stitching on her breast. Heidi. President Chase's girl.

"I love it!" She kissed him again.

"Congrats!" I hugged her again when he let her go.

"Thanks Park, love you." She squeezed me then was pulled away as everyone else hugged her.

"I'm proud of you Chase." I hugged my brother, who was standing with Brax, Sin and Saint.

"Thanks Parker." He kissed the top of my head.

"That poor kid, having you as a father." I teased him.

"Kid has no hope, it's a Greyson." Chase laughed.

"You'll be a good dad, bro." I punched his arm.

"I know. I raised you when dad died and look at you. I fucked up a lot in my life, but not you. The one thing I always had going for me is that I have a kick ass little sister, with the mouth of a fucking sailor and more combat skills than a trained assassin. I love you Park."

"I love you too, shithead." I sniffed and wiped away the tears that formed in my eyes.

He laughed loudly and kissed my cheek, then walked over to Heidi.

"Now that Heidi is pregnant I want her under surveillance at all times." Chase told us, we were all in his office now, after having spent the afternoon and night with the club, having a big family dinner and celebrating Heidi's pregnancy and Mel patching in.

"She isn't to come with us on any missions, I don't even want her leaving the compound without me. We need to keep this info between the club, Thieves Den can't know she's pregnant or the sick fuckers will come after her, especially Trigger." Chase narrowed his eyes as he said the name. "We go about the plan as normal. Tomorrow morning, we head over to the docks, take the guns, kill any and all Thieves Den boys, then get back to the compound. Clear?" He looked at me, Brax, Saint, Sin and Bear, the guy who was replacing Doug.

"Bear and Parker, In want you two together in the building, watching our backs with the security cameras. Sin and Saint, you two will take out the boys waiting for the cargo. Brax and I will sneak on and take out as many guys as we can before alerting Thrash to send down more. Sin and Saint jump on board, we get the guns and go. In and out. No fuck ups." Chase explained.

"Yes boss."

"Make sure the boys are prepped here, that they are ready for an attack, just in case." Chase told Saint and Sin, who nodded.

"Good. Dismissed." Chase hit the gavel and we all got up, walking off. I went straight to Braxton's room and stripped down, pulling on one of his shirts to cover me.

"Could get used to this." He mumbled, standing in the door frame with a smirk.

I rolled my eyes at him and jumped on the bed, kneeling as I watched him. He stepped in slowly and shut the door, pulling his weapons out and placing them on the cupboard without taking his eyes off me.

"You spend most nights in here now." He observed.

"That a problem, convict?" I smirked at him.

"Not at all. But if I didn't know any better, I'd think you liked sleeping beside me." He pulled his cut off and then his shirt as well.

"Who would've thought a big bad boy like you would be so cuddly?" I retorted.

"Such a fucking smart ass." He chuckled.

"We both know that's your main draw to me."

"Mmm, you have so many things that I'm drawn to." He placed his hands on my hips and slowly peeled his shirt off my body.

I laughed and leaned forward, kissing my name over his heart. I unbuckled his belt and pulled his jeans and briefs off so we were both naked, then looked at him.

"Fuck, I'm the luckiest man alive to have you." His deep voice rumbled through his chest as he ran his hands over my soft skin.

"Have me? I'm not yours yet." I smirked.

"You're mine." He said in my ear.

"Fraid not, big guy." I chuckled, clenching my thighs together to ease the throb I felt for him.

"Wanna bet? I'll make you scream it by the time I'm done with you." I shivered at his words and moved to his ear.

"Try me." I whispered.

He picked me up and threw me flat on the bed, kneeling down he placed his mouth on my tattoo and kissed along it, then kissed along my waistline, spreading my legs open wide. He kissed me everywhere, except where I wanted him to.

"Braxton." I whined.

He laughed and poked his tongue inside me, swirling it around and around, making me moan loudly. He backed up and started licking my clit before going back to cleaning me out. My moans got louder and louder and as I was about to come undone, he pulled back and nuzzled my thigh.

"Braxton!" I yelled, reaching out and smacking his head.

"Yeah baby?" He smirked up at me.

"Stop teasing me." I glared at him.

"Whose the only man who can touch you like this?"

"Fuck you." I grinned, willing myself not to give in.

He chuckled and kissed slowly up my body, taking my nipple in his mouth. He caught my hands and pinned them above my head with one hand while the other glided down to stroke me. I cried out as his long fingers entered me and he moved them in and out at a painfully slow pace. I moaned loudly and squirmed from under him, needing more, but there was nothing I could do. He kept up his slow torture, then started to increase the pace, his fingers beckoned, rubbing my G-spot and I cried out as I felt my orgasm, but then he was gone again, completely off of me. Standing beside the bed, he looked down at me as I glared at him.

"Who does this body belong to?" He smirked and cocked his head.

"No one." I panted, my voice shaking.

"You don't sound so sure babygirl?" He grabbed my legs and dragged me over to him, picking me up and placing me on my knees on the bed.

"I don't belong to anyone." I told him.

"You're mine, Parker. You have your freedom and you're your own person, but this body is mine. I'm the only one who can have you this way." He kissed my mouth deeply.

"Not until you make it official." I breathed, my voice wobbly.

"We'll see, Princess." He chuckled and turned me around so I was on all fours on the bed. I felt his tip at my entrance and I moaned brokenly, squeezing my eyes closed.

"Damn baby, you're so wet." He mumbled, slowly pushing inside me, then pulling out. I pushed back against him, hard, making his entire length shove inside me. I yelled out in pure pleasure, feeling how thick and big he was, throbbing inside of me.

"Oh God." I cried out as he thrust into me.

"Say it babe." He ground out.

"N-No." I moaned as he pushed into me at a slow pace, letting me feel him fully.

"Shit, you feel so good." He groaned. This was the second time we had sex, and the first time without a condom after I told him I was on birth control.

"Brax, please. Please!" I begged. The intensity was to much for me.

"Two words, Princess." He reminded me. "Two words and I'll give you what you want." He thrust into me hard for emphasis, making me scream out in bliss.

"Okay, okay! Brax, I'm yours. I'm yours!" I rushed out, pushing back into him. He groaned and increased his pace until he was slamming into me, clutching my hips tightly.

"Holy fuck-" I cut off my sentence as he slammed into me, undoing me completely. I screamed out his name at the top of my lungs as I came, the orgasm made my head spin and my body started shaking.

"Fucking hell Parker!" He stilled inside me and his dick throbbed, then shot his hot release deep inside of me. It seemed to go on forever, then he pulled out and I collapsed on the bed, not physically able to hold myself up. Braxton must of grabbed a wet cloth cause he started to clean me up then pulled his shirt back on my body, placing me in bed properly. He held me to him and kissed me slowly.

"You know I'm yours as well, right?" He told me, his voice vibrated through me.

"Mmmhmm." I snuggled into him.

"Get some sleep babe." He kissed the top of my head and I did exactly as I was told for once in my life.

****


Thoughts on this chapter? What do you think of Chase FINALLY asking Heidi to be his old lady?! About bloody time! Haha

Thank you so much for reading my little sugar cakes!

- Jade xx

# Chapter Fourteen:

I'll face an army

Can't fucking harm me

Out on the front line

That's where you'll find me

- Got Your Six - Five Finger Death Punch

Chapter Fourteen:

Parker's P.O.V

"Fuck!" Braxton tipped his head back as he came inside me while I clung to his shoulders, my fingernails digging into him as I bit down on his neck to muffle my scream. He slowly pulled out of me and placed me firmly on the ground so I wasn't wrapped around him.

The shower water pelted down on us as we gasped for air and Brax cleaned off his dick.

"Can I shower now?" I laughed.

"I suppose." He chuckled and kissed me quickly as he stepped out the shower and wrapped a towel around his waist. I quickly washed myself and rinsed out the conditioner that had been in my hair when Braxton barged into my bathroom and fucked me against the wall. I got out and dried myself off, going into my room where the culprit himself was sitting on my bed in nothing but his jeans and leather cut, cleaning his guns and getting the ready.

I pulled on a blue underwear set and turned to my wardrobe, catching Brax, mid way through reloading his handgun, staring at me.

"Such a perve." I rolled my eyes at him.

"Have you seen your body? Can you blame me? I spent eight years in the pen babe, I've got a lot of perving to catch up on." He smirked.

"Well wipe your drool, it's not attractive." I looked at him, my smirk matching his.

"I'm always attractive, drool and all." He leaned back and winked at me, looking like a Greek fucking God with his abs on full display.

I stuck my finger up at him and strutted into my wardrobe, hearing his laugh as I pulled on my dark jeans and grey tank top. I riffled through the wardrobe again and groaned.

"Whats up?" Brax mumbled, standing right behind me.

"I can't find my fucking cut anywhere. Chase will kill me if I'm not wearing it when we go intercept the shipment." I frowned, looking around. "Where the fuck is it? I hardly ever take it off." I threw clothes around and screamed out in frustration. Now I had just made an even bigger mess, turning my wardrobe into a floor-drobe.

"He's going to murder me." I turned to Brax, who had disappeared. "Fucking convicts. They are like ninjas." I growled to myself as I threw on my motorcycle boots, closing the floor-drobe door behind me. Out of sight, out of mind, right?

Brax was standing beside the bed, staring at me with caution.

"Why do you look like I'm about to feed you to the dogs?" I raised an eyebrow.

"Parker.. I fucking suck at this shit." He chuckled and ran his hand through his hair.

"Spit it out, dipshit." I sighed and smirked at him.

"Shut up, I'm serious." He laughed, then sobered. "Parker, we have a lot of history. A lot of history. We had something real eight years ago and I never stopped thinking about you, just like you didn't with me. Now, we are here and I'm not making the same mistake again."

"Brax, what the hell is this?" I asked, utterly confused.

"Would you shut up for two God damn minutes!" He growled then ran his hand over his face. "God, you frustrate me, woman." He muttered.

"Anyway. What we have is rare, especially for people in our line of work. What we have is something normal people struggle to find. Chase is my brother, the club is my family and I'm sick of looking at your cut, so I took it from you awhile ago and made some adjustments." He nodded to the bed where a black box sat, wrapped up with a red bow.

"Holy fuck." I mumbled, walking over to it and picking it up, ripping the ribbon off and grabbing the cut, I threw the box to the other side of the room, making Braxton laugh at my carelessness. I held up my cut, it was exactly the same, but over the breast pocket were the words I'd wanted to see for the past ten years of my life. Parker Greyson. Queen of the Knights. V. President Braxton's girl.

"Holy mother of fuck." I ran my fingers over the stitching. It was unique to any other patch, showing I was Brax's woman, but I was also Parker mother fucking Greyson, Queen of the club.

"Park, you're fucking killing me. Are you going to just stare at it and mumble fuck over and over or are you going to give me an answer?" Braxton sighed in annoyance.

"You want me to be your old lady?" I looked up at him.

"Of course. You always have been in my mind. I want to officially have a reason to kill any cunt who looks at you." He smirked and my heart melted as I laughed breathlessly.

"I know Chase and Sin did this.. Differently. They said much sweeter shit but you know me babe, I'm the furthest thing from romantic there is. I wanted to do it when it was just us, alone." He mumbled, looking at me.

"I love it. This is perfect. You are perfect." I grinned and tossed the cut on the bed, jumping up into his arms as I wrapped my legs around his waist.

"So, yes?" He caught me and his grin matched my own.

"Of course!" I laughed and crushed my lips on his, kissing him deeply. Our tongues twisted together and we kissed with such raw passion that it left us breathless as we pulled back, our foreheads touching.

"I fucking love you, Princess." He mumbled huskily.

My heart hammered in my chest and I melted into him, turning to goo. The words sounded so good coming from him. He loved me. He loved me.

"Parker?" Braxton chuckled.

"I love you too, Brax." My voice was so soft and full of emotion that it didn't even sound like me.

He grinned and kissed me again, both of us so wrapped up in each other and this moment.

"We need to go." He mumbled against my lips, sounding unimpressed by that fact.

"I know." I replied, catching his bottom lip between my teeth. He groaned and held me tighter, the bulge in his pants pressing against me.

"We need to stop or I'm not letting you leave this room." He pulled back and placed me down on my feet.

I laughed and grabbed the cut, pulling it on.

"You have no idea how long I've wanted to see this on you." He mumbled, running his fingers over the stitching.

"Not as long as I've been waiting for it."

He grabbed my chin and kissed me again, gently this time.

"You're my past, my present, and my future." He told me as his big hands cupped my face.

"I like that." I smiled at the words.

"Me too." He grinned and kissed me once more, then pulled back, taking his cut off and pulling on an armor vest, then a black shirt. His pulled his cut back on and shoved his weapons away. I did the same and pulled my hair up into a messy bun, then we walked downstairs together.

Heidi was grinning like a mad woman and Chase held her at bay while she bounced around. The rest of the guys were all there as well, smiling up at us. Mel stood with a huge grin, cuddled into Sin. Everyone looked to be bursting with happiness except for Candy and the other club whores.

"What's going on?" I frowned in confusion.

"Seriously man?" Braxton muttered to Chase.

"I kept it a secret, but I made the mistake of telling this one. Who told the whole club." He laughed and looked down at Heidi.

"You knew about this?" I looked at Chase.

"Of course. You're my baby sister and he's my best friend." Chase chuckled and pulled me into his arms.

"Congrats baby." He mumbled into my hair.

"Thank you." I laughed and hugged him back.

"Let her go!" Heidi complained.

"She's ours!" Mel tuned in right beside me. Chase pulled back and I was viciously attacked by the two girls.

"It looks amazing, Parker!" Heidi squeaked, looking at the stitching.

"Yeah, yeah. Get off me." I gasped for breath as they held me.

They both laughed and pulled back as I straightened my cut and glared at them.

"You love it." Heidi winked at me.

"No, she loves Braxton!" Saint yelled, making everyone laugh.

"Ugh, this room is to happy and cringe-worthy for me right now." I shuddered. "All of you ease up before I put a bullet through one of you just so it brings down the mood." I teased.

"That's my girl." Braxton laughed, putting his arm around my shoulders and kissing my hair.

"Alright guys, you know the plan. We will be back soon." Chase called out as he pulled Heidi into his arms.

Mel jumped on Sin, the worry evident on her face as she held him like a damn spider monkey.

"I'll be fine babe, chill." Sin chuckled.

"Ugh, I wish I could come." Heidi looked at Chase in envy.

"No fucking way." He narrowed his eyes at her.

"Just be careful, kay?"

"Love you both." He kissed her head and stroked her stomach.

"You too, be careful." Heidi looked at me.

"Always." I smirked as Bear walked over to me.

"You are all sickening." Saint rolled his eyes at the couples, but he had a twinge of jealousy in his eyes. He didn't have that. He didn't have a girl who was worried about him.

"Ugh, Saint, baby please be careful!" I said dramatically, throwing my hand over my heart.

"I do what I want, bitch. Don't try change me." He shot back then burst out laughing.

"How are you single?" I laughed as well.

"It's gotta be the BDD." He shook his head.

"The what?" Mel turned to look at him.

"Big dick disease." He winked as she blushed and Sin chuckled, kissing her head.

"More like boring dick disorder." Heidi smirked at him.

"You two hang around each other to much." Saint narrowed his eyes and pointed between Heidi and I.

"You love us, Saint." I jumped on him and he groaned in pain as he caught me.

"Yeah you do!" Heidi jumped on him as well and he fumbled to catch her as well.

"Get off me you two annoying little smurfs!" He growled, his arms straining.

I placed a sloppy kiss on his cheek and Heidi laughed, tipping her head back.

"Get down you two, we have to go." Chase laughed.

Heidi hopped down gracefully and then Saint dropped me completely, making me fall to the floor.

"Ow! What the hell was that for?" I scowled up at him.

"I couldn't do it with Heidi, she's pregnant." He smirked as I got to my feet.

"Asshole." I rubbed my tailbone and looked at Braxton who was laughing loudly beside me.

"You're all dicks." I muttered and walked outside, climbing into one of the black Range Rovers. Bear got in beside me and I watched as Brax and Chase climbed into an identical black Range Rover, Sin and Saint doing the same in another one. That way, it would be impossible to know who was in what car. Chase went first, me behind him and Sin behind me. We all drove to the docks and parked the cars, getting out.

"Two guys in the camera room. Should be easy to take out. Parker and Bear, when you're in, tell us what you see." Chase said, his voice hard and in charge. Brax grabbed me and kissed me, his excitement for the job showing as his tongue stroked mine.

"Be careful." He whispered.

"You too." I looked at him breathlessly.

I walked off with Bear then turned around quickly.

"I love you." I called back to him. "Don't get arrested this time, okay?" I added with a smirk.

"Love you too. I promise." He grinned as Sin punched his shoulder at the declaration.

I laughed and turned around again, walking over to the security room. I stood on one side of the door, Bear at the other.

"One. Two. Three." I mouthed, then we burst through the door, one gun pointed to each man. We both pulled the triggers and both men slumped to the ground, blood pouring out onto the floor.

Silencers were a fucking blessing.

"Camera guys are down." I said, putting my earpiece in so we all had a direct line of communication. "Bear, move the bodies." I mumbled as I checked the camera feed.

"Okay we got two Thieves Den scum at the entrance to the ship and a guard is there as well. If you shoot them quickly, you should be able to knock them into the ocean." I told them.

"What can you see from the ship" Chase asked.

"Not much." I admitted, trying to zoom in the focus to see anyone aboard the ship. "Couple of guys scattered around but you'll have to be on guard."

"Sin, Saint, go." Chase said.

I watched as they entered the shadows and looked at each other, not even needing to talk. Those two had weird twin super powers. They both shot the two Thieves Den guys in the head and Saint took out the guard before he could even process anything. They both kicked the bodies into the ocean and then Brax and Chase came into view.

"Nice job boys. Make sure no one gets on this boat. Sin, bring the car around." Chase said into the mic. "Parker, watch what you can."

"Yes Boss." We all said.

"Lets go, brother." Chase held his fist out and Braxton bumped it, pulling out his gun.

"Guy on the far right edge, get him in the head and he'll fall overboard." I said quickly. Sure enough, a second later, the body fell into the water.

"Four guys armed on the left, steer clear." I scrolled through the cameras and directed them to the guards I could see.

"That's all I can do guys." I sighed after a few minutes.

"Thanks Park." Chase said into the mic.

I watched as Sin backed the Range Rover up and go out, leaning against it casually.

I clicked back over to see Chase and Brax carrying out the guns. A group of four guys coming towards them. They were going to get spotted.

"Chase, Brax, get down!" I said into the mic.

Nothing.

"Chase! Braxton! Get down!" I yelled.

They couldn't hear me.

Shit.

****

*Evil laughter*

What do you guys think of this chapter?!?! This is my first time writing an action scene, even though it is kind of just a lead up, so I'd love to hear your thoughts!

Thank you so much for reading my little sponge cakes!

- Jade xx

# Chapter Fifteen:

------------------------------------------------------------

H eroes always get remembered,

But you know legends never die.

Emperors New Clothes - Panic! At The Disco

Chapter Fifteen:

Parker's P.O.V

"Parker, whats going on?" Saint asked carefully.

"Get on board! They are going to get spotted!" I barked and jumped up, running on board the ship with Bear. I followed Saint in front of me while Sin waited in the car as our getaway.

We ran around the corner just as the four men saw Chase and Brax.

"Hey dickhead!" Saint yelled, grabbing everyone's attention toward us. Chase and Brax dropped to the floor as Saint, Bear and I all shot at the guys, dropping them all.

"Help the guys." I ordered to Bear, who ran over to help Chase and Brax.

"You, with me." I walked over to the hallway with Saint on my heels.

"Guys we got company." Sin's voice came through into my ear.

"We need to go!" I shouted.

"One each boys. Saint, Park, cover us." Chase barked. The three guys lifted the big barrels and I walked ahead of them as Saint lagged behind, covering our ass.

I put my gun in my jeans and ripped open Chase's barrel, grabbing an AK.

"What the fuck are you doing?" He yelled.

"Subtlety is off the cards now." I explained, tossing one to Saint. I flipped the switch and loaded it easily, pushing the door open.

I heard Saint shoot some guys from the back and I lifted my gun, shooting three guys who were climbing aboard.

"Clear." Saint called to me.

"Clear." I added.

"Guys hurry the fuck up!" Sin yelled. I ran off the boat and took out more guards, clearing the path with Sin backing me up while Saint watched the guys' backs.

"In, in, in." Sin opened the back of the Range Rover and the guys threw the guns in the back.

"Let's go!" Brax yelled. "Park!" He grabbed my arm and ripped me behind his body as he aimed and shot at a guy rounding the corner.

"Fuck, we're being ambushed. We need to get out now." Chase yelled, jumping in one Range Rover with Saint and Bear while I jumped in the other with Sin and Braxton. Brax put his foot flat and we sped out of there, leaving the third Range Rover behind.

"Saint, Chase, Bear? Any of you copy?" Sin asked into the mic piece.

No response.

"Fuck!" He yelled, slamming his fist into the dash.

"We got company." Braxton mumbled.

I spun my head around to see three bikes and a car chasing us down.

"I got it." I snuck into the back with the guns and I grabbed another two AK's, tossing them up to Sin.

"What's your plan?" Braxton asked.

"Run them off the road before they run us off the road." I mumbled.

"That's it?!" Sin screamed.

"So far." I mumbled and lay on my back, sending my boot into the back side window, pushing it out.

"Jesus fucking Christ." Braxton muttered.

"Keep it steady." I yelled over the wind that blew through the car. I slowly leaned out the side and aimed the AK, hitting the trigger and sending bullets everywhere but where I wanted them.

Fuck, man, this looks so much easier in movies! I thought as I pulled back in.

I slowly did the same thing, leaning out and aiming the gun. I took a deep breath and shot, slower this time. One shot hit the windscreen of the car, cracking it. I reloaded the gun and heard gunfire as Sin leaned out and did the same thing.

"One bike, down!" He called out.

I cocked the gun and sent a bullet into one of the bikers heads, killing him and knocking him off his bike. The car ran over the body as the bike spun off the road and I aimed again, shooting out one of the cars tires.

It lost control and swerved to the side of the road, falling into a ditch, making it roll over, around and around.

"Biker and car are down." I announced.

"Fucking hell!" Brax yelled. I spun to look at him, but his eyes were ahead of us. I looked up and my jaw dropped. Bullet holes coated Chase's Range Rover as Saint drove like a bat out of hell. There was no sign of Bear and Chase himself was halfway out the backseat window, being dragged by a man in a car alongside them.

"Chase!" I reloaded the gun and came up front, gripping the dash.

"Bikes down. How the fuck do you suggest we help with that though?" Sin asked, coming back into the car.

"Buckle up." Braxton mumbled.

"What??" Sin and I looked at him.

"Buckle up!" He yelled.

I fell into the backseat and pulled my seat belt on as Sin did the same.

"Be just my fucking luck to die as soon as I get Mel." Sin grumbled.

"Relax." Brax ripped up the handbrake and the car did a 180 so we were facing towards Chase's car and the other one.

"You aren't about to do what I think you're about to do!" Sin shouted in disbelief.

Brax threw the car into gear and shot forward.

"Fucking hell, you are. We are so fucked." Sin breathed.

"Not yet we aren't." Brax ground out, his eyes straight ahead as we came closer and closer to the car.

The car started furiously honking it's horn and then it all went into slow motion. Chase turned and saw us right there, his eyes going wide as he sent his fist into the guy holding him, breaking free and trying to pull himself back into the car.

The other car swerved out of our way, flipping over at the force of it, landing on it's side, making our car scrap against it as we flew past.

Brax slammed the brakes on and spun around, grabbing the AK, held it out the window and shot the gas tank to the car as he went past. He changed gears smoothly and peeled around the corner and an echoing explosion ripped through the air, making the ground shake.

Silence filled the car except for all of our heavy breathing and then we saw Chase's car up ahead, at a stop probably doing the same thing.

"You two are made for each other. You're both fucking psychos." Sin muttered breathlessly.

"Are you okay?" Braxton turned to look at me, his eyes going all over me, checking for injuries.

"Just shaken up. You?" I whispered.

"I'm fine." He reached back and placed his hand on my leg as he slowly drove over to Chase's car. We all climbed out as Saint opened the door and hugged his brother.

"You okay?"

"I'm fine, bro, you?" Sin clapped him on the back.

"I'm fine." Saint pulled back and hugged Brax and I.

"Where's Chase?" I snapped, ripping the back door open.

"Parker, don't freak out." Chase looked at me evenly. Blood covered him and all of the backseat.

"What the fuck happened?! Where's Bear?" I asked frantically. Then my eyes landed on him, in the very back of the car, bloody and still.

"Oh fuck." I covered my mouth and looked at Chase.

"They got him." Chase pulled me into a hug as tears left my eyes.

"Jesus Christ." Sin mumbled.

"You're bleeding." I observed, feeling my top get wet.

"The car pulled to the side and shot Bear. I went to shoot them but they grabbed my gun and used it to pull me out the car. When I wasn't coming out as easily as they hoped, the guy cut me. I'm fine, it's not deep. That's when you guys showed up." He looked at Braxton.

"You saved my fucking life bro." Chase hugged him.

"Anytime, brother." Braxton hugged him back.

"Show me the cut." I said.

"Parker-"

"Show me." I demanded.

Chase sighed and lifted his shirt, exposing a slice in his side.

"Shit." I mumbled. Sin took his shirt off and held it against Chase's side firmly.

"I'm fine." Chase ground out.

"Just take it." I snapped.

"We need to go. Cops will be here any second." Braxton looked around nervously.

"Meet at the compound." Saint climbed back into the car with Chase, Sin sliding in with him just in case. Braxton grabbed my hand and we jogged back to the car, getting in and speeding away.

"You were amazing back there." Braxton rested his hand on my thigh.

"So were you." I held his hand in mine and kissed his knuckles gently.

"You've really become a soldier now." He glanced at me with a smile.

"You need to be on top of your game when you're a girl in a mans world." I shrugged.

"You're fucking amazing. Most guys want some innocent, sweet girl. But you're perfect. You're so strong and smart. You think fast and do what needs to be done. You take no shit from anyone and speak your mind. You're incredible. I love you." He leaned over and kissed my cheek.

"Love you." I looked at him and grinned as we pulled into the compound.

Heidi and Mel sprinted out of the mansion, running over to the cars. Heidi looked pissed, Mel looked like she was crying. The other brothers followed them outside, looking concerned.

"Chase Greyson I'm going to fucking slaughter you!" Heidi screamed, not knowing which car he was in.

We all climbed out and Mel breathed a huge sigh of relief, jumping into Sin's arms, seeing he was okay. Chase slowly got out and Heidi's anger dropped, turning to worry.

"Oh my God, babe." She ran to him and hugged him tightly.

"We saw the news, about the explosion and we didn't know what to think." Mel sobbed into Sin's chest.

"Come on babe, lets get you inside to check on Chase." Sin angled his body so she couldn't see Bear's dead body within the car.

"Where's Bear?" Heidi mumbled, looking at us all.

No one answered.

"Oh fuck." New tears ran down her cheeks and she hugged Chase.

The other brothers looked down in sadness and hugged those closest to Bear.

"Heidi, we need to get Chase looked at." I pried her off my brother and she clung to me, crying. "I know, honey. I know." I stroked her hair and looked at Brax. He nodded and helped Chase inside with Sin and Mel.

"I'll handle Bear." Saint said glumly.

"Clean him up to be buried." I told him as I pulled Heidi inside.

"I need to see Chase. I need to be with Chase." Heidi cried.

"Okay, let's go." I walked her into the lounge room where Doug was propped up on the couch, looking at Chase with worry. Chase was lying on a table that had been pulled in here with a bottle of whiskey in his hand. Braxton was at his side while others crowded around and Mel did her thing. Braxton and Sin explained everything that happened while Chase breathed deeply, his eyes staring at the ceiling with his jaw clenched as Mel worked on him.

"All done. Be careful you don't rip the stitches." Mel told him.

"Thanks doc." He mumbled, taking a swig of whiskey.

"Those fuckers." Victor mumbled when Brax and Sin were done.

"We will get them back. Today was a success, all things considered." Chase grit out.

"Get out there and help Saint with Bear." I told Victor.

"Yes boss." He looked at me and quickly walked away.

"Parker.." Axel, one of the guys looked at me, tears in his eyes.

I raised an eyebrow at him.

"Whose going to tell Tracey and Anna?" He asked.

Fuck. Bear's ex wife and daughter.

"Oh my God. Parker he had a daughter!" Heidi gasped, bursting into new tears. Pregnancy was really fucking this girl up.

"Heidi." I growled at her.

"Here, Parker, I've got it." Mel grabbed a sobbing Heidi and helped her up to her and Chase's room.

The guys looked after her in shock. Heidi was normally like me, we got shit done. She was never a crying mess because the boys relied on us to be strong. Heidi and I were the glue.

Chatter erupted from the guys, some of it was comfort to those close to Bear, some was declarations of revenge and some of it was worry about the club. I quickly jumped on the coffee table and stood up straight.

"Right, listen up!" I shouted, making everyone look at me and a silence to fall over the room.

"What happened today, shouldn't of happened. It was a quick job, in and out. But we were ambushed. They knew would our move would be. Losing Bear is a tragedy. He gave his life for the club, for you, for your families. Tracey and Anna will be notified and we will all attend Bear's funeral. We lost a brother tonight. A friend. We lost family." I stopped and looked around at all the grim faces.

"But we can't afford to be weak. We need to see their next move and then strike. This is war. I want all of you training daily. Guns, combat, everything. We need soldiers. Are you soldiers?" I cocked my head to the side.

"Yes boss." They called out.

"Of course you are. You're Knights. You're not weak. So get a beer, get a girl and do your thing tonight. Because from here on out, you will eat, sleep and train. Now get out of here!" I waved my hand and they applauded, with a few hoots. I laughed and watched as they left the room and then the music started, the bass pumping through the house.

"That was a hell of a speech." Chase said in a tight voice.

"Someone needed to say it." I smirked down at him and hopped off the table, going to him.

"You did well babe." Braxton threw his arm over my shoulders and kissed my head.

"Is Heidi going to be like this for the whole pregnancy?" Chase asked.

"Do I look like an expert on pregnancy and motherly shit?" I raised an eyebrow at him.

"Good point. You're a heartless bitch." He chuckled and then winced.

"Which is why I can't tell Tracey and Anna." I said seriously.

"Parker-"

"Chase, I can't. How do I tell Tracey, her ex husband died doing the thing she left him for? How do I tell a six year old that her dad took a bullet to the fucking head?"

"The girls rely on you, Parker. You hold them together. Half the boys' old ladies would of left a long time ago if not for you." Chase gripped Braxton's forearm and slowly pulled himself into a sitting position.

"Me and Heidi. Not just me." I shook my head.

"Heidi can't she's too emotional."

"And I'm not emotional enough!" I yelled, the took a deep breath. "Chase, I know cars. I know bikes. I know fighting and guns and torture. I know how to be a soldier. You raised me to be a soldier, a girl of war. Not a girl who does womanly things." I sighed. "I can't cook to save my fucking life. I sleep with a glock beside me and one eye open. Ask me to pull apart a gun and put it back together and I'm your girl. But ask me to be emotional and talk to a grieving family? I can't."

"Jesus Christ." Chase put his head in his hands. "I keep saying how proud I am that I made you like this.. But you're right. I raised you to be.. Me."

"That's not true." Braxton mumbled.

We both looked at him.

"Parker, yes. You are different to other girls. But that isn't wrong. That's just you. You are a soldier and a fucking good one at that. But, if you think you don't show emotion then you're an idiot."

"What do you mean?" I frowned at him.

"Today, you took the cut. That was emotion. As you walked off at the shipyard you yelled out that you loved me. That's emotion, Park. You shut it out, but you are a caring, beautiful, compassionate woman. You just don't take shit from anyone. And I love that about you." His blue eyes burned into my green ones as he shocked me silent.

"Brax is right." Chase mumbled. "He brings out a lot of emotion in you. Emotion you kept hidden for eight years."

"Ugh, whatever. Point is, I can't tell them." I rolled my eyes and gulped, not wanting to admit the truth.

"Well Heidi can't either." Chase glared at me.

Great.

Heidi had to go and get knocked up and now I'm expected to feel.

Ugh.

****

Hey guys! God, this chapter took me so long to write! It was so difficult and I really don't know why! So, I apologize if the quality is a little shitty :/

What did you think of all the action?!?! :o

Thank you so much for reading my little potatoes! (But real talk, if I had to only eat one thing for the rest of my life, it would totally be potatoes! You can have so many different things! Hot chips, potato chips, hash browns, wedges, roast potatoes. UGH YUM)

- Love Jade xx

# Chapter Sixteen:

----------------------------------------------------------------

S end in the dogs of war

- Dogs Of War - AC/DC

Chapter Sixteen:

Braxton's P.O.V

I am the luckiest man in the entire mother fucking world.

There is no doubt in my mind, Parker was fucking made for me. Crafted by the Gods, especially for me. I don't know what I did to deserve her, but I am eternally fucking grateful.

That sexy smirk and the twinkle in her eye, promising trouble. The way she spoke, swearing like a sailor and having such an attitude. Watching her handle a gun, like it was apart of her hand and how she fought men twice her size, getting knocked around and thrown to the ground, but she always got back up. She is the baddest girl I know, and one of the most dangerous people I know-man or woman.

Every part of her was pure perfection and I fucking loved that girl more than anything.

If anyone could hear these thoughts, they'd probably think I'm being a cute cunt and I'm watching her as she sleeps, her head resting on my chest with a small smile on her face.

But, no. Instead, I was watching her as she danced in front of me wearing a black lace lingerie set with thigh high stockings on and a pair of heels to Warrant's 'Cherry Pie'.

I tipped my beer back, not daring to take my eyes off her as she moved around before she slowly strutted her way over, her long hair flipped to one side as she placed her hands on my knees and winked at me, giving me a fantastic view of her cleavage.

I've said it once and I'll say it again; I'm not a romantic man. I'm a pig.

Parker grabbed my beer and took a big mouthful then handed it back to me, standing up fully again.

She smirked and her eyes lit up and I knew I was in trouble. I watched her perfect round ass as she walked over to the door and grabbed my cut, pulling it on over her small body.

Fucking hell, how did she make it look so good?!

She lit up a blunt as she came back over and inhaled deeply before blowing out a cloud of smoke. I sat and watched as she passed me the blunt and turned around so her back was to me, then she started dancing again.

I groaned and puffed on the joint, as she made my dick throb in my jeans.

When Parker turned back around, she crawled into my lap, straddling me and she ran her hands down my arms slowly as she purposefully bit her lip, knowing exactly what that did to me. I took another hit and leaned forward, kissing her deeply as she inhaled the smoke from me. Her hands went to my chest and she pushed me back, making me make a low noise in my throat and clench my jaw.

This girl was the biggest fucking tease. She blew out the smoke I had given her and started grinding down on me as the song changed to Def Leppard's 'Pour some sugar on me'. I placed my hands on her thighs gently as she moved like a fucking pro, then wrapped her arms around my neck, tilting her head back, her hair tumbling behind her. I kissed her collarbone and nuzzled my face into her neck and she moaned lightly. God, that fucking moan.

Parker ran her hands down my bare chest as I nipped her earlobe, earning another moan from her.

Fuck it. I thought as I stood up and placed the joint into my beer bottle. I held onto her thighs tighter so she didn't fall and she squealed at the change.

"Hey!" She scowled at me.

"I can't handle it anymore. I need you." I mumbled into her ear.

"Brax." She moaned. I swear to fucking God, I've never loved my name so much until I heard her screaming or moaning it.

I moved one hand to pull my cut off of her but she stopped me, smirking.

"What?"

"Put it on." She purred.

I raised my eyebrow and smirked.

She giggled and pulled it off, helping me into it while she was still wrapped around me. I shrugged it on the rest of the way and sent my hand back, snapping her bra and pulling it off to show me her gorgeous tits. My mouth was already around her nipple before the bra hit the floor and she gasped as I bit her lightly. I pinned her against the wall and lifted my head up to her as I reached between us and tore the sexy little piece of fabric from her body.

"Fucking hell, Brax." She meant for it to sound annoyed, but I knew it had just turned her on more. I smirked and stared into her eyes as I pushed two fingers into her, making her eyes flutter and her mouth form an 'o'.

I worked my fingers in and out of her, feeling how incredibly wet she was and she moaned, dropping her head back to rest on the wall. My dick was so hard it was hurting as I watched her orgasm into my hand, crying out my name like a fucking prayer. I slowly withdrew my fingers and sucked them clean as she watched me, her green eyes so bright they were like emeralds.

I wasted no time reaching down and unbuckling my jeans, pulling my dick out and slamming into her, making her scream out, her hands clutching the sides of my cut. I tipped my head back and groaned, feeling her so hot and tight around me as I slowly moved in and out of her.

Picking up her knee from my hip, I slowly pulled it up so it was resting on my shoulder and I thrust into her, hard, over and over, until her moans were screams. I felt her constrict around me and watched as her eyes rolled back into her head as my name left her lips.

I clenched my jaw and let out a string of curses, feeling her come all over me. I caught her lips with mine and kissed her fiercely as I continued to push myself, needing release. Parker bit down on my tongue and I groaned, feeling my dick throb and then shoot into her. A choked sound left me as my orgasm went on and Parker moaned at the feeling.

"Christ Park." I kissed her forehead, both of us gasping for breath.

"Mmm." She nuzzled into my neck and I smiled slightly, slowly pulling out of her and taking her to the bed. I went and grabbed a towel and cleaned us both off then pulled her heels and stockings off as she lay there, exhausted. I pulled my shirt onto her body and took my cut and jeans off, putting on a pair of basketball shorts, I climbed into bed with her and held her to me, falling into a sex coma.

"Have you got any names yet?" Parker asked Chase as we sat at the table.

"Heidi is so indecisive, everyday it changes." He rubbed his stubble and shook his head.

"I heard that you asshole!" Heidi scowled, waddling into the room. She was a lot bigger now, hitting the seven month mark in her pregnancy.

"Hey gorgeous." Chase smiled at her.

"Don't gorgeous me. I look like a mother fucking whale." She grumbled, walking over to the fridge and grabbed out a juice.

"So you don't pancakes and bacon?" Parker smirked and nodded to Mel who was manning the stove.

"Of course I do!" Heidi threw her arms up and glared at her best friend.

"Alright, preggas, chill." Parker teased.

"Parker I will fucking put a bullet in you." She grumbled, sitting down at the table.

"Just cause you're Chase's girl doesn't mean you're top dog around here." Parker smirked.

"Yeah? Trust me, I'm scarier than you when I'm pregnant." Heidi stared at her.

"No, you're so cute!" She jumped up and hugged Heidi.

"Get off me, fat ass. You sure you aren't pregnant?" She groaned even though Parker was the furthest thing from fat.

Parker stopped laughing and death glared her while Heidi laughed.

"Wouldn't fucking surprise me. I vote we move Brax and Parker to a sound-proof part of the house." Doug grumbled as he walked into the room, only having a tiny limp in his step now.

I smirked as I remembered my lap dance and fucking Parker against the wall.

"Come next to ours. You won't have that problem." Chase mumbled.

"Chase!" Heidi squealed, slapping him.

"Fuck, babe I didn't mean-"

"No! Don't even say anything you jerk! I'm carrying a fucking human in me, I'm sorry if I don't want to be fucked twenty four seven! Why don't you just find Candy to do it for you?!" Heidi yelled, stood up, grabbed a plate of food from Mel, then stormed off.

"Smooth." I mumbled as we all stared after her.

"Shut the fuck up." Chase said in a murderous voice.

"How long?" Doug asked with a raised eyebrow.

"I will gut you." Chase moved his glare to him.

"That long?" Doug's eyebrows shot up.

"Two months." Chase mumbled and ran a hand through his hair.

My heart went out to the man. Chase was my brother and I can safely say he hasn't gone two months without sex in.. Well.. Ever. I mean, fuck, I was in the joint and I was getting laid every couple weeks.

"Uh, bro.." Sin walked in with a confused look on his face.

"Yeah?" Chase looked at him.

"Heidi just ran into her old room crying. Thought you should know. I asked what was wrong but she threatened to cut my dick off if I didn't get away from her. Girl is scary when she's pregnant." Sin shook his head.

"Fuck." Chase put his head in his hands. "I fucking suck at this shit. I don't even know how to have a missus and now I need to be a dad as well."

Parker rolled her eyes and got up, going over to the freezer and grabbed out a tub of cookie dough ice cream with a spoon.

"Here." She handed them to Chase.

"Parker, it's nine in the fucking morning. I don't want ice cream." He glared at her.

"Not you, you fucking idiot." Parker whacked him over the head with the spoon, making him scowl and rub the spot.

"Heidi's pregnant. She's doubled in size and her best friends are still as sexy as ever." She turned and wink at Mel, who giggled and blushed. "She has known you forever, she knows what you're like. She doesn't feel good enough for you, especially when you make stupid comments and she has to see those whores all over you every time she turns her back. This is her favourite flavour of ice cream. Go." Parker shoved it in his face again.

"Parker, maybe your heart isn't as icy as we thought." Doug said in surprise.

"I got laid last night, I'm in a good mood." She turned to smirk at him.

"You get laid every night. Trust me, I'd know." He shuddered.

"Hence why I've been in a good mood!" Parker laughed.

I laughed as well and watched as Chase got up, grabbing the tub and spoon.

"Thanks, love." He kissed her cheek, took a deep breath and walked off.

"Heidi needs to realize she looks gorgeous with her little baby bump." Mel smiled, putting the food on the table.

"Least Brax knows how to handle you when he knocks you up." Sin laughed, coming over to sit down.

"Oh please. I know I'm a Queen." Parker joked, pointing to the stitching on her cut. "Says so right here. Plus, that's where Heids and I are different. She would get upset and pissed off seeing a girl all over Chase and wreck all his shit. I'm different." She shrugged, popping a piece of bacon in her mouth.

"What would you do?" Mel cocked her head to the side.

"I'd put a bullet between the eyes of whatever stupid slut touches him." Parker said evenly.

"God, I've been living here for four months and I'm still not used to how brutal you are." Mel chuckled.

"That was tame, for her." Doug laughed.

"Parker's a psycho." Sin shook his head.

"She sure is." I pulled her over to me and kissed her lips, hard.

"Do you think you will try get pregnant soon, Parker?" Mel asked, making Parker choke on her spit.

"Hell no! I just got him back after eight fucking years." She looked at me and kissed my jaw, wrapping her arms around me.

"Yeah. Just us two for awhile." I agreed and held her tighter against me.

"But you want kids?" Mel pressed.

"The only thing I want right now, is to win this war with my brothers against Thieves-Fucking-Den." I mumbled.

"I agree." Parker laughed as I shoveled an pancake in my mouth.

"And after that?" Fuck, did she ever give up?

"Who knows." Parker shrugged.

"In this life, especially in Brax and Parker's positions in the club, having a normal family is hard." Sin explained.

"How come?"

"Cause normally, the man handles the club business and the wife handles the kid. And Brax and I are both leaders in this club. No maternity leave in an MC, sweetheart." Parker leaned back into her chair and kicked her feet up, looking cool and calm. "Plus, I could die tomorrow. I could get shot up and so could Brax. With this war, it's possible we die. Or go to prison. Our life is more complex and we all know I'm not mother material." She continued.

"Sin's in the life and I want to have a kid one day." Mel looked a little nervous and Sin choked on the bacon he was stuffing into his face. He turned red and punched his chest to dislodge it while Doug and I smirked at him.

"Thanks for the help assholes." He wheezed when his airway was clear.

"Don't plan things." Parker said, looking directly at Mel.

"Huh?"

"Don't plan anything. It's how you get hurt in the end. Just take it day by day." She shrugged and stood up.

"Parker has a point." Doug nodded.

Mel looked down and Sin sent her a look that made her roll her eyes.

"Mel, I just meant that this life is different. Sin isn't a normal guy. You need to understand that."

"Yeah, yeah I get it, Park." She smiled, got up and slowly left the room.

"Morning fuckers." Saint walked in wearing a pair of jeans and nothing else.

"Walk of shame." Parker smirked, looking behind him.

"Only if I'm ashamed." The girl Saint had been screwing for about a month walked in with blonde hair so messy, it was dreaded. Black makeup smudged her face and she was wearing a small top and those yoga pant things that show the perfect shape of a girls ass and legs. I thanked whatever God was out there everyday for those things.

"Looking classy as ever, Diamond." Parker laughed.

"Classier than you."

"Enough. Diamond get out." Saint rubbed his hair.

"Okay baby." She skipped over and ran her hands down his chest. "Call me later?"

"Maybe." He leaned back on the counter and she kissed him quickly, before walking right back out.

"That girl is trouble." Parker shook her head.

"That girl also has no gag reflex." Saint turned to smirk at her. The guys and I laughed as Parker turned up her lip.

"Well I'm out of the doghouse." Chase said, walking in with a giant grin.

"Looks like that's not all you got." Doug mumbled.

"I got a blowjob." He said proudly.

"Ugh! Sister ears!" Parker groaned, throwing her hands over her ears.

"I'm calling church." He laughed and walked right out. I got up and picked Parker up, tossing her over my shoulder.

"Braxton!" She squeaked, punching me in the back.

"Ugh, can you stop yelling out his name? I've heard it enough over the past few months to last a lifetime." Doug muttered as he, Sin and Saint followed us up to Chase's office.

"Not her fault I'm a sex God." I smirked.

"Okay, stop. That's my baby sister." Chase groaned, appearing ahead of me. I laughed and pushed him out of the way as I walked in the room and collapsed on the chair, pulling Parker down to sit in my lap. She scowled at me and moved in my lap so she was leaning against my chest with her feet kicked up on the table.

"I've got ears and eyes all over the place and there hasn't been a peep from the Den. It's been months since the run in with the shipment and.. Nothing." Chase sighed, falling into the chair beside me.

"I don't feel good about it." Sin frowned and shook his head.

"Something's brewing." I agreed.

"But no one knows what." Chase growled.

"We need to make sure the information that Heidi is pregnant stays under wraps. Trigger will go crazy if he finds out." Parker mumbled.

"Fucking idiot." Saint shook his head.

"That's another thing. Trigger's mine. I want to be the one to put a bullet in his head after everything he put her through." Chase's eyes turned dark.

"I want Thrash." I said in a cold voice.

Parker looked up at me.

"He threatened Parker. Said he would claim her as his own and rip away all she has built. He was going to whore her around and keep her as a slave. That cunt is mine. People need to know she's mine and I won't tolerate threats to my girl." I clenched my jaw as my blood boiled.

"I want a piece of that." Parker added. "After all, I was the one who got the threat." She shrugged.

"Couples that brutally torture and kill together, stay together." Saint muttered.

"I'm going to be a dad in two months. I need to get this shit done. I can't have this war going on when my baby is born." Chase shook his head.

"Bro, that kid will be the most protected person in the club." I reached out and clapped him on the back.

"I know." He breathed out a slow breath.

"So lets kill these cunts within two months. Get ready boys." I grinned at the rest of them, feeling the familiar excitement of a war coarse through my system.

****

I figured, we haven't heard from Brax for awhile, so why not!

This chapter is, obviously, a few months in advance, just for progression purposes :)

I just wanted to say a HUGE thank you to one of my good friends on Wattpad, Willow! We are so tight, we even have a ship name (it's Jalow, btw) She is crazy talented and such a sweetheart! Go over to her profile and give her some love! Thank you so all your support girly! xx

Thank you so much for reading my little gumdrops!! :)

- Jade xx

# Chapter Seventeen:

------------------------------------------------

I am,

Living the dream

I am,

What you fear most

I am.

Anarchy.

- The Pride - Five Finger Death Punch

Chapter Seventeen:

Parker's P.O.V

"What about Zach for a boy?" Heidi asked Chase as Brax and I walked into the room that would be for the baby.

"Not Zach." Chase shook his head.

"Josh?" Heidi cocked her head to the side.

"Definitely not Josh." Chase narrowed his eyes.

"You're so difficult! Why the hell not?" Heidi threw her hands in the air.

"I've killed a guy named Zach. And Josh. I'd rather not name my kid after someone I murdered." Chase looked at her.

"Jesus Christ, by that logic, the kid will never have a name." Heidi mumbled.

He smirked and winked at her.

"What if it's a girl? Chase hasn't killed many girls. Only when absolutely necessary. That's usually my job." I shrugged.

"Yeah. But it's trying to find a girls name that he hasn't fucked." Heidi glared a hole into my brothers head as he ran a hand through his hair. Braxton laughed knowingly and I turned my lip up.

"To my defense, not even I remember half of their names." Chase offered.

"Wow. Congratulations, Chase, you giant slut!" Heidi snapped at him.

Chase thought for a second. "What about Jay for a boy?"

"Jay.. Sounds good bro." Braxton tested it.

"Not Jay." Heidi and I said at the exact same time.

"Why?" Chase glared at us both.

"What colour are we painting this room?" I clapped my hands and looked at Heidi, ignoring the holes that we being burned into our heads by the boys.

"Baby blue." Heidi smiled and held up a paint tin.

"Okay, but I'm not coming back in here to re-paint if the baby is born a girl." Braxton grumbled.

"You'll do what I say.." Chase smirked, causing a playful fight to break out.

"Girl or boy, I like blue. Fuck society and their gender colours." Heidi used quotation marks. "Break it up. If either of you put a hole through the wall, I will kill you both myself."

"Yes boss." Chase smirked and lay one last hit on Braxton before backing up.

"Grab a brush." Heidi told us.

"Looks good guys." Mel smiled, coming into the fully painted room while we all lounged on the floor.

"Thanks." Heidi grinned.

"Any luck on a name?" She cocked her head.

"Nope." Heidi slumped against Chase.

"What about Layla?"

"Christ, not Layla." Braxton groaned.

I looked over at him with a raised eyebrow.

"Yeah. Not Layla." Chase agreed.

"I don't even want to know." Heidi shook her head.

"Carli?" I suggested.

"Carli.. Have you fucked a Carli?" Heidi looked at Chase.

He thought about that, then grinned. "Not to my knowledge."

"Did we just pick a girls name?!" Heidi's eyes lit up.

"I think we did." Chase smiled.

"Chase!" She turned and hugged him tightly.

"Carli is such a beautiful name!" Mel nodded, a huge smile on her face.

"And Parker picked it!" Heidi turned to me.

I smiled and hugged her.

"Congrats guys." Braxton kissed Heidi's cheek and punched Chase's shoulder.

"You guys are going to make amazing god parents!" Heidi squeaked, then slapped her hand over her mouth.

"Fucking hell Heids, one job." Chase groaned.

"God parents?" I raised an eyebrow.

"It was meant to be a secret until the kid was out." Chase laughed.

"Parker, you're my best friend. You're Chase's little sister and Braxton is Chase's best friend, his brother. We want you two to be the God parents." Heidi rubbed her tummy.

I shared a look with Braxton, then looked back at Heidi. "We'd love to." I grinned, pulling her into a hug.

"Thanks bro." Brax mumbled to Chase.

There was a click and we all looked up to see Mel with her camera.

"So cute." She giggled, wiping a tear away.

"Ugh, I need to leave before I throw up over how lame this room is." I said, wiping away a sneaky tear.

"Don't act like you aren't insanely excited." Chase laughed, pulling me into a bone crushing hug.

"Shut up." I smiled and hugged him back.

"I'm hungry, let's go eat." Heidi sighed.

We all walked downstairs together and went into the kitchen where Sin was stuffing his face with pizza.

"Sin! I told you to wait!" Mel swatted him.

"I'm hungry babe!" He said around a huge bite of pizza, pulling her into a hug.

"Hey guys." Saint walked in with a new girl on his arm. She was blonde and perky with big blue eyes. She looked like she belonged in a place like hooters. Chase, Braxton and Sin all froze, in a trace as they looked at her. Saint grinned in pride.

"Hey." She smiled and waved, looking a little intimidated with all the giant men gawking at her chest.

"Don't mind them. They are just giant pigs." Heidi slapped Chase's chest and he snapped out of it, looking down at her. Braxton shook himself and looked over at me, where I was leaning against the counter with my arms crossed, smirking at him. He shot me a guilty smile and I laughed, shaking my head as he came over and held my hips, kissing my head.

"I love you." He mumbled.

"Love you too." I smiled and got on my tip toes as he leaned down to kiss me gently.

"So this is Parker and Brax. Chase and Heidi. Sin and Mel." Saint said lazily.

"I know who they are." She winked at the guys and smirked.

"Right." Saint shrugged and walked over to Sin, grabbing a slice of pizza and shoving it in his mouth.

"I didn't realize you had a girl, Sin." She cocked her head to the side.

"Yeah, Mel and I have been together a few months now." Sin pulled her closer to him and she smiled.

"Shame. Us three could of had a lot of fun." She smirked at the brothers. Saint choked on the pizza and Sin's lip turned up in disgust as he looked at her.

"Yeah well, to bad." Heidi snapped at her, seeing Mel shrink down into Sin's chest like a scared puppy.

"Heidi.. You look.. Pregnant."

"You little-" Heidi started but Chase grabbed her and held her against his body.

"You should leave now." I glared at her.

"Parker. Still trying to be a woman in a mans world, I see. That's cute."

"Say what you want, sweetheart. Everyone knows and fears Parker Greyson. I have respect and power. What do you have?" I smiled.

She narrowed her eyes at me.

"Get off my property." I added with a wink.

Her mouth opened, then closed, then opened again. Like a fish.

"Did I fucking stutter? Leave now or I'll get one of my boys to carry you out in a body bag after I put a bullet in those tits you have paid so much for." I pulled out my gun and cocked it, pointing it at her.

She gulped and nodded. "I'll go."

"Good idea, honey." I grinned as she walked out.

"Doug. Follow her. Make sure she leaves." I put my gun back in my pants and Doug silently followed her out.

Braxton wound his arms around me, standing directly behind me, he nuzzled the back of my neck and I could feel a familiar hardness in his jeans. "God you're so fucking hot." He groaned quietly, kissing my shoulder.

I laughed and turned in his arms, snaking mine around his neck. He kissed me deeply and pressed me tighter against his body, his tongue peeking into my mouth.

"Ugh. Stop." Chase growled.

I felt Braxton's hand leave my body and I leaned back slightly to see him holding his middle finger up at my brother. I laughed and backed up as Braxton smirked at Chase, then we all sat at the table, eating pizza.

"So, that was Carli." Saint laughed.

"What?" Heidi looked at him blankly.

"That girl." Saint waved his hand.

"Her name is Carli?" Chase added, glaring at Saint.

"Yeah.. Why?" Saint frowned.

The four of us looked at each other.

"Not Carli." We all said at the same time.

"Saint, I hate you." Heidi threw a slice of pizza at him and he looked at us all in confusion.

Chase's phone rang before anyone could say anything and he sighed, picking it up.

"Whats up?"

He sat upright in his chair and looked at Braxton and I.

"Who is this? Hello? Fuck!" He jumped up.

"Baby?" Heidi looked up at him.

"Knights! We need to leave, now!" He yelled, his voice booming around the house.

"What happened?" I stood up.

"Thieves Den are at the bar. Gunning down everyone in sight. Got an anonymous tip."

Victor ran in with a bag full of stuff, throwing it on the table.

"The cars are being loaded up with weapons now." He rushed out. Saint ripped open the bag and the guys all pulled their shirts off, putting on vests.

"Parker, you're with us. Saint, you're in charge here. Look after the girls." Chase said as he pulled his guns into their holsters.

"Yes boss." Saint nodded and started barking instructions to the brothers who were standing at the ready.

Mel kissed Sin deeply and Heidi looked at Chase, holding her big belly, her eyes tearing up.

"I'll be fine baby girl. I promise, I'm coming home in one piece to both of you." He kissed her, then kissed her belly.

"I love you." She sniffed.

"I love you too, babe."

I pulled my top off and strapped on a vest, pulling the top back on and slipping my cut on over it. I loaded up all my weapons and stuffed them into my paint stained clothes.

Braxton kissed me deeply, catching me off guard, his lips urgent and full of passion, taking my breath away.

"I love you so fucking much." He mumbled, his blue eyes burning into my green ones.

"I love you, Brax." I breathed.

He kissed me once more, then straightened, staring out at the guys. "Let's go to fucking war."

****

I know the last few chapters have been kinda on the uneventful side, but you all knew this was coming!! WHO IS EXCITED?! I KNOW I AM!

Only a few chapter left guys! I hope you're ready!

I'm just going to quickly add in here, if you are liking this story, why not go check out my other works? I have 6 altogether on my profile and I'd love for you guys to read my other stories while you wait for another update ;) If you are one of those loyal, fabulous people who HAVE read my other stories, I want to thank you, so much! It honestly means so much to me and I love that my stories bring people some joy and happiness! It's an incredible feeling :) Thank you ALL! <3

Thank you so much for reading my little pumpkin pies!

- Jade xx

# Chapter Eighteen:

I'm a fucking soldier

Just like I told ya

While I'm just warming up

You're getting colder

Out on the battleground

Let's take a look around

Well there's a million of us ready to throw down

- Got Your Six - Five Finger Death Punch.

Chapter Eighteen:

Parker's P.O.V

"I'll take one side with Sin and the boys. Brax, Park, you two take the other side with your group." Chase said, pulling into an alleyway.

"Chase." I jumped out of the car and jumped on him. "Please, be careful."

"You two, little sis. Stick with Brax. I love you." He hugged me tightly.

"Love you." I squeezed him, took a deep breath, then backed up, squaring my shoulders, I put my game face on and turned around, facing the other brothers as they pulled up.

"Half with me and Sin. Half with Braxton and Parker. Shoot to kill, boys." Chase said to them all.

"Good luck brothers." Braxton added.

They split up and we went in different directions, Brax and I took the back while Chase and Sin took the front of the club. Music was still pumping, but that was the only sound, it was eerie. Gunfire rang out from the front and Braxton swore, ripping open the door and rushing in, taking out two guys.

We all flooded inside and took cover behind walls, gunfire all around us. I clutched my AK and spun around the corner, raining bullets into the backs of four guys that were shooting at Chase and Sin.

"Behind us!" One of the Thieves Den guys yelled, making half of them turn, their guns pointed at me. A hand gripped my forearm and I was yanked to Braxton's body, behind cover.

"Be fucking careful you crazy woman!" He whisper yelled at me as bullets fired where I had been standing.

"I needed to get their attention off Chase and the guys." I looked up at him.

"Not by attempting suicide, baby." He sighed and pulled me behind him. He grabbed a Sawn-off shotgun from the back of his jeans and he shot one guy in the head, blowing his brain all over the wall as the body slumped to the floor.

"They are pushing us. Hold position and take them out!" Brax called back to the guys.

I reloaded my AK as Braxton continued taking people out with his shotgun. He pulled back to reload and a guy rounded the corner his a rifle pointed at Braxton's chest. I booted him in the hip, sending him to the ground and fired into his face, killing him instantly.

"Thanks, babe." He looked at me, loaded in the last shell and flicked it back into place, firing a few shots off around the corner.

We made our way out with Braxton and I leading the others. Bodies scattered the floor and I looked up to see Sin with a guy behind him.

Chase plunged his knife into the back of the guys neck, severing his spine and he slumped on the floor.

"That all of them?" Braxton looked around, confused.

"Looks like." Sin scratched his head.

"That was it?" Doug frowned from beside me.

"Something isn't right." Chase's eyes scanned the place furiously.

"Thrash and Trigger aren't here." Braxton looked at Chase.

"If we were at war.. They would be here.." He frowned and looked stumped.

"Is everyone okay?" I looked at both of the groups.

"Fine on our side." Chase looked over his men.

"Ours too." Brax muttered.

"This doesn't add up!" Sin sent his fist into the wall. "Why have a war with this many men! Why have a war without the two bosses?"

I rubbed my head and walked over to some of the dead bodies, kicking them on their backs so I could see there faces, or at least what was left of them.

"No one familiar." I yelled back to them as I kicked over the last body.

I turned to walk back out to them, but I was wrenched against a hard body.

****

Braxton's P.O.V

"No one familiar!" Parker called out to us as she went and checked the bodies.

"What the fuck then!" I ground out.

"Oh fuck." Sin muttered. I looked up at him to see his eyes huge. Chase looked furious. I followed their gaze and rage and fear spiked through me.

Parker was staring right at me, her body held tightly against a man dressed in all black, including a ski mask. He held a hunting knife to her throat and his hand covered her mouth.

"Let her go you cunt!" I jumped over there but I felt arms go around me, yanking me back. I fought them off as my brothers tried to keep me at bay, my eyes trained on Parker.

"What the fuck do you want?!" Chase yelled. I glanced over to see him in the same position, being held back.

"Parker Greyson." The man mumbled, ignoring us. He spun her in a slow circle and his eyes raked over her body. Over my girl.

"You're a very gorgeous woman, Parker."

"I'm going to tear you to fucking sheds." She growled.

"So feisty. Is she like that in the bedroom, Braxton?" He looked at me.

I lunged again but couldn't shake off all the guys.

"Dude, brother. Stop. He'll hurt her. You need to relax." Doug told me in a low voice. I sighed and shook them off, holding myself back.

Chase did the same, he must of been given the same speech.

"I bet she's wild." The man droned on.

Parker spat directly in his face and he sent his fist into hers, catching her before she fell and pinning her against a wall.

"Don't fucking touch her! What do you want?" Chase yelled.

I couldn't hear or see anything, but then, he turned with her in his arms, her lip was bleeding where he hit her.

"You guys think you're so untouchable. The Knights will be in pieces by the end of this." He told us.

"Please just let my sister go!" Chase begged.

"I was under strict orders not to.. defile her. Thrash has strict orders about what happens to little Parker. But he'd never know." The sick fuck ran his hands over Parker's body and she snapped her fist into his face, knocking him back. She turned to run, not having any of her weapons, but before anyone could think, he had her again.

"Big fucking mistake sweetheart." He told her in a hard voice.

I watched in slow motion as he pulled her hunting knife out of his jeans and sent it into her side. Parker made a choking noise, looking down, then he tossed her to the floor, running out.

"Parker!" I screamed, running over to her and falling to my knees.

"After that cunt now! I want him alive!" Chase yelled out as he dropped down with me.

"Parker, baby girl, no. No!" I held her to me, her head in my lap as tears ran down my cheeks.

"Brax." She whimpered.

"I'm here baby." I looked down at her.

"It hurts." Her eyes locked on mine.

"I know, but you gotta stay with us, Park." Chase kissed her face and ripped his shirt off, holding it against her side.

"I.. I'm tired." She fluttered her eyes closed.

"No! Parker don't you fucking dare leave me! Don't you fucking dare!" I yelled, my arms and chest sticky and warm with her blood.

"I'd.. Never.. Leave." She whispered.

"Stay awake baby girl! Stay with me! Parker!" I screamed brokenly.

"We need to go. Now! She needs to get back to the compound or she'll die!" Sin's voice floated to me and I gently lifted her in my arms, making her whimper.

"You'll be okay, Princess. You'll be okay." I repeated over and over as I made my way to the Range Rover, holding her to me and pressing Chase's shirt into the hole as Chase and Sin jumped in, driving like a bat out of hell.

# Chapter Nineteen:

-------------------------------------------------

S tay with me, don't let me go

Because there's nothing left at all

- Ashes Of Eden - Breaking Benjamin

Chapter Nineteen:

Heidi's P.O.V

I chewed on my nails and tried to focus on the baby names Mel was droning on about. She had suggested it to take our minds off all the people we loved who were at war.

"Kami, Kara, Kally."

A kick from within me made me stop her.

"What?" She looked up from the online baby girl names.

"Go back. What did you say?" I looked down at my big belly.

"Kami?"

"No, the other one." I waved my hand as the guys turned to watch what we were doing.

"Kara?"

"No!" I rubbed my belly gently.

"Kally?"

The baby kicked.

"Do you like the sound of that little one?" I laughed breathlessly, rubbing both hands over my stomach.

"Kally.. I like it!" Saint grinned.

"Little baby Kally." Mel kissed my tummy.

"I'll need to check with Chase.. But I love it. Now I just need boys name." I scowled.

Mel, Doug, Saint and I were all sat in Chase and my room with me lounged on the bed, my back killing me. The TV was turned on with minimum volume, just in case we caught sight of something that was off. Saint had sent the other guys to patrol the compound and wait for the others to return. Mel had prepped all her medical equipment for the worse case scenario. That girl was fitting in so well around here.

"God, I'm so worried." She mumbled, staring at the TV.

"We all are." I sighed. "But they have most of the brothers over there with them to back them up. Parker, Sin, Brax and Chase are all amazing at what they do."

"Do you have some weird twin connection to Sin?" Doug looked at Saint.

He shook his head, looking at Doug like he was the most idiotic man he had ever met.

"Do you know Sin's real name?" I looked at Mel, curious.

"Do you?" She raised an eyebrow.

"Of course. He got drunk and told me when I was eighteen." I laughed at the memory. He had told me it was a huge secret and I wasn't to tell anyone.

"Yeah, I know." She smiled.

"What is it?" Doug spoke up.

"You don't know?" Mel looked at him.

"Nope. Or Saint. What are your real names?" He cocked his head.

Saint smirked.

"I don't know Saint's." Mel stared at him, curious.

"I do." I looked at Saint and smiled.

"What is it?" Mel asked.

"Yeah, what is it?" Doug stepped closer to me.

I made a show of zipping my lips and throwing away the key.

"Fuck sake." Doug grumbled. "I'm going to go grab some food." He walked off and Saint watched after him, then looked at Mel.

"Cole. My real name's Cole." He smirked.

"Cole and Kaden." Mel pieced it together with a smile.

He laughed and came over to the bed, placing his hand on my belly.

"C'mon kid, you could at least boot your mumma for me." Saint mumbled, a cheeky grin on his face.

"Shut up jerk." I laughed and shoved his shoulder.

"I can't wait till the kids born. You and Chase will make good parentals." He moved his big hands around my stomach and the baby kicked his hand, making him jump ten feet in the air, and me groan in pain at the force.

"Fucking hell!" Saint looked up at me. "Are you okay?!"

"I'm fine. The baby just kicked." I laughed at his reaction and placed his hand back on my belly.

"That's so crazy. Hey kiddo! I'm your uncle Saint. Now, you're going to hear a lot about uncle Sin being the most attractive one, but I'm telling you now, I'm the hot one." Saint started talking to my belly.

Mel and I laughed as he went on and on about how he was the most attractive guy in the Knights and he would be the favourite uncle.

The door burst open suddenly and we all snapped our heads up.

"Oh shit." One of the guys mumbled, staring right at me.

"Heidi?! Baby girl?!" That voice.. No..

All the blood drained from my face as Trigger burst into the room and laid eyes on me.

Saint jumped up and pulled my body behind his, grabbing his gun he took out the guy beside Trigger, killing him. Then he aimed at Trig.

But he wasn't fast enough.

Trigger lifted his handgun and shot Saint in the head, making him fall back and hit the carpet with a thud.

"You stupid bitch!" Trigger screamed at me. "You're having that pathetic assholes baby?!"

"Trigger." I breathed, my body frozen with fear.

"I can't take you looking like this." He said to himself. "Fuck! Heidi you ruin everything!" He sent his fist into the wall.

"This was going so well! Luring the others into what they thought was war and then coming here and snatching you! But I can't do that when you're pregnant!" He yelled.

He raised his gun and shot at me before I could even process what was happening. A sharp pain filled my chest and I looked down, seeing blood pour onto my shirt.

I looked up in time to see Trigger run to the window and climb out. Doug shot and got him in the arm, then he was gone.

"Heidi!" He screamed.

My legs gave out but I was caught by Mel. She was talking to me but I couldn't hear her. It was like white noise, my eyes were locked on the lifeless corpse of one of my best friends, my brother. A red pool trickled all around Saint's head, thick and sickly.

Saint. Cole. He had died for me. For my baby. Oh God. My baby.

Chase was there then, covered in blood as tears ran down his face. He was yelling at me, begging me. But I couldn't hear any of it.

"Baby.. Save.. Baby." I tried to get out.

More tears left Chase as Mel came back into my vision, getting to work at trying to fix me.

"Chase.. Baby.. Cole." I got out, then my eyelids fell closed.

www.ingramcontent.com/pod-product-compliance
Lightning Source LLC
Chambersburg PA
CBHW070344200726
48294CB00003B/775